Triple Crown Publications
presents

BITCH

Reloaded

D1055742

by
Deja King

Compilation and Introduction copyright © 2007 by
Triple Crown Publications
PO Box 6888
Columbus, Ohio 43205
www.TripleCrownPublications.com

Library of Congress Control Number: 2007928280
ISBN: 0-9778804-7-8
ISBN 13: 978-0-9778804-7-8
Associate Editor: Chloe Hilliard
Editorial Assistants: Elizabeth Zaleski, Nazlihan Kavak
Editor-in-Chief: Mia McPherson
Consulting: Vickie M. Stringer

First Trade Paperback Edition Printing July 2007

10 9 8

Printed in the United States of America

BITCH

Reloaded

This Book is Dedicated
In Memory Of:

Kia D. Smith a.k.a. Caramel_diva07

I had the pleasure of meeting you only once at the Harlem Book Fair but I'll never forget your warm spirit and beautiful smile. You may no longer bless us with your presence but you're very much alive in the hearts of many.

Acknowledgements

This book is strictly for readers, book vendors, book clubs and retail stores who support my work. When I created the character Precious Cummings, I had no idea so many of you would gravitate to her...thank you and I love you for that!!

Tureko "Virgo" Straughter, girl thanks for the push. Telling me you needed the sequel "Now" gave me the motivation to knock this story out. Ms. Monalisa, my MySpace partner in crime; I love you girl. Sunshine716, I love for you to read my books before they hit the streets because you give it to me raw with no chaser. Tazzyt2bossye, thank you for being a cheerleader for me as an author and honest at the same time. Andrea Denise, am I really your favorite author? (smile) Girl, you are too sweet for words. For the booklovers who reach out to me and show me love on the message boards, thank you. Chocolate Girl, Cikeithaia, Clarity, Super Woman, Lady Scorpio, Sarah Todd, Shoshana Chanel, Jocelyn Carter, Ssavon Russell, Tanisha Pryce, Nicole Garner, Carl J. Northrop, Laurie Bowman, Myra Green, Travis Williams, Brittney and Sexy Xanyll. For everyone I forgot to mention please forgive me. My memory is shot out and I have ADD, but you know I have nothing but love for you!!

To the naysayer who doesn't understand the title Bitch Reloaded or Bitch. It stands for: **"Babe In Total Control of Herself"**. There isn't anything negative about it. In pop culture, think Alexis from Dynasty and Amanda from Melrose Place, the word Bitch is worn as a badge of honor, representing a confident, powerful woman who is in control. Only in urban culture, due to many men in the hip hop industry using it in a negative light, do people find it derogatory. I used the term Bitch as a way of taking that power away from men because I'm a female and I wouldn't title a book to describe a woman that I found offensive. So open your mind and enter the world of Precious Cummings, you might enjoy it!!

For everyone who has assisted with bringing this project to life—thank you. Special thanks to my editor Chloe Hilliard. Special, special thanks to Miss Jones of Hot 97 for being one of the first to embrace Bitch and promoting it on your radio show. Keith Saunders of Mariondesigns, thank you for blessing me with a second book cover that is hotttt!! Last but certainly not least, I want to show love and respect for Vickie Stringer and the entire TCP family.

Much Love,
Deja King

Most importantly, to my readers, I hope you enjoy reading this book as much as I enjoyed writing it!

Deja King

Preface

The Present...

It's been said that every time a child is born, someone has to die. I prayed at that moment that someone wouldn't be me.

"Push, I need you to push, Precious," the doctor ordered. I had been in labor for what seemed like a lifetime.

"I can't fucking push no more. I been pushing all fucking night. Now here it is, the morning, and this baby still don't wanna come out," I said, damn near in tears.

"I know you're overwhelmed and in a lot of pain, but I can see the baby's head. One more push and it will all be over with."

"Doctor, you been saying that shit for the last couple of hours. Now is the head coming or going, which one is it?" I screamed breathlessly, ready to beat the doctor and the nurse's ass. I was on the edge of becoming delusional. This was not how I imagined childbirth. The girls in my hood always made it seem that after you got your epidural it was smooth sailing, but that wasn't the case for me. My mind and body were drained, and all I wanted to do was fall back and go into a deep sleep.

"Doctor, we're losing her. Her vitals are weak," said the nurse.

"We might have to perform a cesarean." The doctor couldn't hide his fear. "If we don't do something both mother and baby will die."

I could hear the commotion in the room as my mind began drifting off. My life started flashing right before my eyes. All the hell I had caused and endured. The many battles I'd fought—some I'd lost, but many I'd won. This here was the biggest battle of all, saving the life of me and my unborn child. It seemed as if I was leaving my body and my mind was taking a journey back in time. I began reminiscing about the road I'd traveled that brought me to where I was right now, some of it good but most bad. With all the pain and heartache—would this be how my life ended? Would my last breath be in a hospital giving birth to the baby I wanted more than anything else in this world?

Love for Life

The Past...
Summer 2006

They say a cat has nine lives. Although many describe me as having feline characteristics, the skill of escaping death seemed to be what we shared most in common. Less than two hours ago, Nico left me for dead with a bullet to the chest, and when my eyes closed that is exactly what I believed my fate would be. As my husband Supreme cradled my limp body, begging God to let me live, someone up above must have heard him because here I was still holding on. My body seemed to be in another place, but my mind was perfectly coherent and I could hear the chaos that was going on around me. A male voice yelled, "Clear the area! Prepare this patient for emergency surgery."

"Yes, Doctor," a lady replied. The atmosphere was hectic, and all I could think about was Supreme and the baby that was growing inside of me. I wondered where he was and if he believed I would survive.

"The bullet entered the right anterior chest, perforated the lung and is lodged in the right lateral chest wall. If we don't remove the bullet immediately she will die within the next few hours," I heard the doctor explain to his staff. The nurse must have given me medicine to numb my entire body, because from the conversation I knew they were operating, but I didn't feel any pain.

I was still in shock, not grasping that Nico tried to take me out. He didn't hesitate when he pulled the trigger; his eyes were dark and cold. I guess the same way mine looked when I was about to leave a nigga leakin' by the curb. If I survived this knock on death's door, I would have to contemplate what my next move in life would be.

After replaying in my mind Nico pulling the trigger and feeling the heat burn a hole in my chest over and over again, I heard the doctor say, "Make sure the wound is completely drained before I close the incision." *Does that mean the procedure was a success and my people's final visit to see me wouldn't be in black suits?* Before I could find out the answer to that question, I lost consciousness.

"Baby, can you hear me?" Supreme asked as I slowly came out of my daze. His face was blurry, but his signature diamond-encrusted medallion was like a bright light flashing in my eyes. My vision soon started becoming clearer.

"Supreme, is that you?"

"Yeah, baby, I'm right here."

"Our baby!" I reached for my stomach, but Supreme grabbed my hands and brought them up to his face.

"Ssshhh, we'll talk about that later," he said placing my hands on each side of his face. "You're still weak and it's touch and go. The doctor believes you should make a full recovery, but you have to relax."

"I can't believe I pulled through. I thought this was it for me," I said, straining my voice.

"We'll talk about all of this later. Just get some rest. I promise I'm going to stay right here with you day and night until you get outta here." Supreme kissed me on my forehead, and I knew that meant our baby wasn't as lucky. Nico got his wish...well sort of. He did take my life—at least part of it. I fell back asleep because knowing that the future I wanted so desperately was no longer growing inside of me was more than I could bear.

For the next four weeks I basically slept, rested and had physical therapy twice a week to help regain my upper body strength. Just as he promised, Supreme never left my side.

"Good morning." I had just woken up and as always, Supreme was the first thing I laid my eyes on.

"Hi, baby. How are you feeling?" Supreme asked while holding my hand.

"A lot better, especially waking up with you beside me."

"I told you I wasn't going nowhere."

"I know, but I'm ready to wake up with you beside me in our own bed, not this stinky-ass hospital room."

"I see your sassy attitude is coming back. That must mean you're close to a full recovery," Supreme said with a slight laugh.

"You got that right. I'm ready to get the hell outta here. Plus this hospital food is about to give me a crack head body. You so worried about following the doctor's orders that you won't even sneak me in no jerk chicken or rice and beans. This shit is for the birds, baby, I'm ready to go."

"I feel you. It was going to be a surprise, but the doctor is making arrangements for your release as we speak."

"What! I'm leaving today?" I screamed, ready to snatch off the rinky-dink green smock and hit the front door.

"Calm down, more like tomorrow afternoon."

"Thank ma'fuckin goodness. Another day in this place was gonna make me postal."

"We can't have that. I don't want to take no more chances

losing you."

"Especially since we lost the baby," I said, turning our light conversation serious.

"Precious, we don't have to talk about the baby."

"Supreme, how long do you plan to avoid it? I know I lost the baby and I'm sick about it. This child meant everything to us."

"It did, but I'm so grateful that I didn't lose you, too. That's something I would never have gotten over."

"The first thing I want to do the moment the doctor gives us the green light is start creating another baby. This time we'll make sure it's protected."

"No doubt. Nico Carter will never have the chance to take another child of mine."

"Baby, what's going on with Nico? Have you heard anything?"

"Besides the police, I hired three different private investigators to hunt him down. No one has seen him. They're thinking that maybe he was able to get out of the country. But don't worry, Nico is far away and won't be able to hurt you again. Wherever he is hiding, my men will find him. He's already dead and doesn't even know it."

Since being in the hospital, that night was the first night I fell asleep without Supreme by my side. He said he wanted to make sure the house was perfect for my arrival, and he was the only one that could guarantee that.

"No, no, no!" I yelled waking up in the middle of the night. My body was drenched in sweat and my hands were shaking. I immediately picked up the phone and called Supreme.

"Hello," Supreme said in a muzzled voice.

"Baby, wake up, it's me."

"Precious, is everything a'ight?" he asked, waking up out of his sleep.

"I just had to hear your voice. I had the worst nightmare. I dreamt that Nico showed up at the house and shot you dead. It seemed so real."

"Baby, I'm fine. I've added extra security. It's like Fort Knox up in here. Nobody is getting in, especially not Nico. I'll be there tomorrow to bring you home. Now get some sleep. I love you."

"I love you, too." I closed my eyes breathing a sigh of relief that Supreme was alive and well. It was definitely time for me to leave this hospital because it had my imagination running wild.

The next day, Supreme greeted me with a huge bouquet of flowers and the most adorable pink baby doll dress. My perfect size six frame was down to a zero, so Supreme went and purchased me a new wardrobe to accommodate my drastic drop in weight. I was going to enjoy stuffing my face to gain the pounds back.

"Precious, you look beautiful," Supreme said as I stepped out of the bathroom. With my hair pulled back in a long pony-tail I looked liked a black Malibu Barbie.

"Thank you, baby."

"I have something else for you." My eyes lit up as Supreme pulled out a Jacob the Jeweler box.

"What is it?"

"Open the box."

"Damn, this shit is so hot," I said, gazing at the pink dia-mond heart-shaped necklace.

"Read the back," Supreme said, turning the heart over. The engraving read: *S&P Love for Life.*

"The moment we get home, the first stop is the bed-room," I whispered in his ear, and then our lips met and our tongues explored each other as if it was the first time. My whole body tingled when Supreme embraced me.

"That's if we make it to the bedroom." Supreme smacked my ass. "Now let me put your necklace on."

"Baby, this is so beautiful, I love it."

After Supreme put my necklace on me, he put his hands around my waist as he sat down on the hospital bed. He pulled me between his legs and stared into my eyes. "Precious, I love you more than anything in this world. Nothing or no one will ever come between what we share. Whenever you doubt that, just hold on to this necklace and know my heart will forever belong to you."

"I don't know what I did to deserve you, but I'm just happy you're mine."

The nurse came in and brought in the wheelchair. Although I was perfectly fine on my feet, it was standard procedure for all patients to be escorted out in that manner. Supreme pushed me down the hallway and a smile spread across my face knowing I was just a few feet closer to freedom. The automatic doors opened and Supreme kissed my forehead as the afternoon sun welcomed us. The summer was coming to an end, but it was still slightly hot and not a single cloud was in the sky.

The Suburban was parked right out front with his bodyguards posted beside it. As my shoes touched the cement, my eyes caught a glimpse of a black van slowly approaching the entrance with its window rolled down. Before I could lock gazes with the passenger the ringing of a machine gun spraying bullets filled the hot summer air.

"Precious, get down!" Supreme barked as he threw his body on top of mine to cover me. All I heard were the screams of innocent bystanders as the shooter tried to finish me off, not caring who lost their life in the process. The bullets finally ceased and the van disappeared as quickly as it appeared. Supreme's bodyguards ran toward us with guns drawn, but the attackers were long gone.

"Supreme, are you okay?" I asked trying to move from beneath his heavy body. I didn't get an answer. My back and neck felt warm and wet, but it still wasn't registering until I heard the sobs from Supreme's bodyguards.

"Oh shit, they took my man out!" yelled Nathan, Supreme's head of security. Gently, the bodyguards and doctors, who rushed to us once the gunfire stopped, lifted Supreme off of me and laid him face up on the ground. To my horror, his chest was riddled with bullets. My whole body began shaking as I stood over my husband unable to speak. Doctors tried to find a pulse, but it was too late. Supreme was dead and there was no saving him.

My body buckled, I fell to my knees and balled my fist to the sky. "Damn you, damn you, why did you take him away from me!" If there was a God, I hoped he heard my cry. I knew I had done a lot of fucked up shit in my life, but I didn't deserve this. I threw myself over Supreme, wanting to feel him one last time. I wanted to breathe life back into him, but he was gone. His blood saturated my dress as I held his face and glided my fingers over his lips and whispered, "Love for Life."

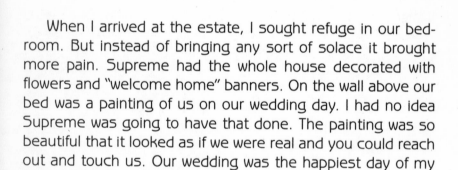

Black Widow

When I arrived at the estate, I sought refuge in our bedroom. But instead of bringing any sort of solace it brought more pain. Supreme had the whole house decorated with flowers and "welcome home" banners. On the wall above our bed was a painting of us on our wedding day. I had no idea Supreme was going to have that done. The painting was so beautiful that it looked as if we were real and you could reach out and touch us. Our wedding was the happiest day of my life, and today was the saddest.

Entering Supreme's closet, I started to hug and smell his clothes. His intoxicating scent briefly softened the pain eating away at me. I curled up in the fetal position and cried until no more tears were left.

A few hours later I was awoken by pounding on my bedroom door. I pulled myself off the closet floor and walked to the door still wearing the pink baby doll dress now soaked in Supreme's blood. In my mind I never wanted to take it off because with it on I felt a part of him was still with me.

"What is it?" I yelled before opening the door.

"Precious, it's me, Nathan. The police are here to speak to you."

"Tell them to come back later."

"They need to speak to you now. Precious, you have to do this for Supreme," Nathan said, sounding choked up. He was right. I didn't like to fuck with the police, but anything to help bring down my husband's killer.

"Okay, tell them I'll be down in a few minutes." I wanted to get myself together before I spoke to the officers. I knew Supreme would want me to be strong. I grasped the diamond heart around my neck and found strength in that. After changing my clothes and washing my face I went downstairs.

A couple police officers and a few bodyguards were in the dining area of the kitchen, surrounding the plasma screen television and listening to the news.

"Early this afternoon, superstar rapper Supreme, born Xavier Mills, was gunned down in front of The Valley Hospital in Ridgewood, New Jersey as he exited the facility with his wife, Precious Mills, who was being released after suffering her own brush with death last month. Doctors pronounced the twenty-four-year-old dead at the scene. Police are still looking for the suspects, who witnesses say drove off in a black van with New York license plates."

"Cut that off," I said calmly. Everyone turned around and looked at me with pity in their eyes. The more pity I saw, the straighter I stood. One thing I detested more than weakness was pity, because pity was a sign of seeing weakness in someone else. I never considered myself to be weak and didn't want others to see me that way either.

"Mrs. Mills, I'm sorry for your loss," the pudgy white male detective said as he walked toward me. I just nodded my head in acknowledgement. "Can we go somewhere and talk?"

"Sure, just a moment. Anna, please bring me a Hennessy and coke; I'll be out back," I instructed the maid. "Would you officers like anything?"

"No, we're fine." I knew I had no business drinking in front of the police, since I was not of the legal age, but I didn't give a fuck. This was my house and my husband was dead. If I wanted to pull out a vial and snort a line of coke it wouldn't be any of their business. Luckily drugs weren't my thing.

As I sipped my second drink, I caught myself yawning as the officers did more idle talking than revealing any new facts. "So it seems you all are no closer to tracking down Nico Carter," I said, growing increasingly tired of their bullshit.

"We're not a hundred percent sure Nico Carter is responsible for the death of your husband."

"Excuse me. The motherfucker pumped one in my chest a month ago, leaving me for dead and he came back today to try to finish where he left off. But instead he killed Supreme. You tryna say there is no connection? Well, I have a hole in my chest that says otherwise."

"We're just saying we need to look at all the facts. There haven't been any sightings of Mr. Carter, and your husband was a very successful rapper. We want to make sure this wasn't a hit from one of his rivals."

"You have to be fuckin' kiddin' me. I know you two rent-a-cops ain't tryna turn this into some rap war. Y'all ain't 'bout to spin my husband's death into Tupac and Biggie, Part 2. This ain't got nothin' to do wit' rap. This is about my ex-boyfriend stuck on revenge, period. Don't be wasting time investigating niggas that ain't got nothin' to do wit' this. Go find Nico Carter, and you'll have your killa."

Just like that, I went from victim and widow to cold-blooded bitch from Brooklyn. The lady I spent that last two years trying to become took a back seat to the ride 'til I die bitch that was still in me.

"Thank you for your cooperation, Mrs. Mills." Closing their notepads and rising from their seats, the detectives didn't know how to react. "We will continue to investigate and keep you abreast of any new developments. Once again, we're sorry for your loss."

"Hum hmm, I'm sure you boys can see yourselves out," I said, sitting back in my chair admiring the landscaping of the acres in our backyard. I looked at the pool, remembering the time Supreme and I went skinny- dipping in the middle of the night. It was the first time I ever had sex under water. I stared at the basketball court where he faithfully played Sunday afternoon games with his friends.

I clasped my hands over my mouth as I went into deep thought. I had to figure out a solution to this problem. There was a trail of dead bodies left behind due to me and Nico, and it had to stop. The only way to make that happen was to finish Nico off once and for all. If only it was as easy as it sounded. I had been away from the streets for so long that I didn't know who was making what move. But one thing never changed in this game: Money always talks and bullshit always walks. I had access to endless amounts of cash and I would use that to get all the information I needed.

I went upstairs and retrieved my cell. I flipped it open and went to contacts. I found my man Smokey's number and dialed him up. After four rings he finally answered, "What up?"

"Smokey, what up, this Precious."

"*The* Precious?"

"Yeah, nigga, what's good."

"Damn, from what I hear, nuttin' for you."

"I tell you what, why don't you come see me so you can tell me all about it."

"Where you live?"

"In New Jersey. I know it's a little far for you, but under the circumstances I can't leave my house. But I promise I'll make it worth your while."

"When do you want me to come?"

"Now. This can't wait."

"I'm on my way." I gave Smokey the address and let the security know to expect him. When I lived in BK, Smokey was a small-time dude who I used to cop weed and my heat from. He also kept his ears to the streets and knew everything that was going on in the hood, for a price of course. Normally I didn't like to bring my street dealings to where I lay my head, but at this point in time my home was the safest and only place to conduct business.

Wanting to look as relaxed and in control as possible, I let my hair down and put on some lip gloss and a knee-length white linen shirtdress. When I went back downstairs Anna had finished preparing the meal I requested. The table was set outside and everyone knew not to disturb me unless they heard me screaming bloody murder. I wasn't too concerned since Smokey would be triple-searched before he even gained entrance through the gate, and guards would be posted at every entrance.

"Precious, your guest has arrived," Nathan said as I sat outside.

"Thank you, escort him back here. Also tell Anna she can bring out the dinner."

When Nathan brought Smokey out he still looked the same, except for having put on an extra ten pounds or so. Since he was a lil' nigga an extra ten pounds on him actually looked like twenty. His eyes were still glassy, so I knew he smoked a blunt before he came in. That's where he got the name Smokey from, because the nigga stayed lighted up.

"What up, Precious? It's good to see you," he said giving me a hug.

"It's nice to see you, too, have a seat."

"Damn, ma, you done real good for yourself. Word is born, you living like straight royalty."

"Except I no longer have my king."

"Yeah, I'm sorry about that Precious," Smokey said as he looked down, shaking his head. "That's why I was surprised you called me. That shit just happened today and you already on top of yo' game. I don't know how you holding it together."

"Smokey, that's why I'm in this fucked up position now, because I let shit slip. I took it for granted that other people would make sure Supreme and I would be protected instead of being on top of shit myself. Now my husband is dead and I'm a widow, make that a black widow, 'cause I fucked up. I'll never make that mistake again."

"So how can I help?" Smokey asked.

"First, you can tell me what the streets is saying."

"Word is born, everybody was initially hollering about Nico putting a bullet in you. They couldn't believe that nigga just got out the dusty and came knocking at your door. His lawyer got him off on that Ritchie shit, but he was definitely going down over you. We was like that nigga is slippin', leaving witnesses and shit."

"I don't know if he's slippin' or if he caught a case of bad luck. He definitely didn't expect for me to survive or for Supreme and his bodyguards to show up and ID him. So what else?"

"Everybody is wigging out over Supreme's death. That nigga was a legend. He was a young cat, but already dropped like six CDs. The whole hood is ready to take Nico out. But they also saying he couldn't have done that shit alone."

"You got any names for me?"

"Nah, this shit just happened not even twelve hours ago. You got to let the dust settle. But I will tell you this, while you were in the hospital, people were saying Nico left the country, that he was in Trinidad, Jamaica, or the Dominican Republic. He was ghost out this bitch, so that's why everybody was buggin' out about Supreme's death. We trying to figure out when Nico got back or if he ever left."

"Smokey, I want you to get word out on the streets that there's a million dollar hit out for Nico. But I want the body delivered to me, either dead or alive." Smokey nearly fell out his chair when the words dropped out my mouth.

"Did you say a million dollars?"

"That's right."

"Damn, I might have to kill that nigga myself."

"I don't care who does it, but I want it done. Or they can bring Nico to me, nice and bound, and I can finish him off. How it's done is irrelevant to me, as long as Nico is dealt with." I pulled out an envelope containing twenty-five thousand dollars and handed it to Smokey.

"What's this for?" he asked, not knowing what was inside.

"It's a little something for your time. I want to make sure my message reaches the streets ASAP. Also keep me informed of any new information that comes your way. Now let's eat."

Long after Smokey left, I lay across our bed staring at the painting of me and Supreme. We were so happy and in love. Our life together was just beginning and in an instant it was over. Here I was living in a fourteen million dollar New Jersey mansion, far away from the gritty streets of Brooklyn, and I still wasn't safe. The streets had followed me home—or maybe I *was* the streets, and there was no escaping them.

Old Friends and Fake Niggas

It took all my strength to get out of bed the next morning. I had been making Supreme's funeral arrangements and finally, it was D-Day. Supreme wasn't even six feet deep yet and attorneys, family members and all sorts of other motherfuckers were coming out the woodwork. See, Supreme didn't leave a will, and since I was his wife, everything was coming to me. I knew he would want to make sure his parents were financially straight, so I had no problem lacing their pockets. But then bitches were stepping to me with kids in all shades, sizes and ages saying they were Supreme's. One chick even managed to get my cell number.

When she called I said, "Listen here, if that's Supreme's seed then he'll be taken care of, no question. But see I don't do DNA tests. So get your blood work together and call my attorney. If your shit is legit then he'll make all the financial arrangements for your little one. But on the real, don't call me no more, 'cause I'm not interested in knowing you or your kid."

I don't know if hood rats think that DNA tests can't be

done on the deceased but they were coming at me hard. I shut all that shit down. I'm not saying Supreme was a saint but he didn't strike me as the type of dude that wouldn't claim what was his. These trick-ass bitches weren't stepping to me when he was alive but now they wanted to dishonor his name in death. Not on my watch.

I stood in front of the full length mirror scrutinizing myself in a black St. John suit and black crocodile Jimmy Choo pumps. That bid in the hospital really did my body in. My ass only had a slight curve unlike its normal round bump. I couldn't stress it, after a few more weeks of Anna's cooking I would be back on point.

"Precious, the car is waiting for you," Nathan said through the door.

"Okay, I'll be there shortly." I grabbed my black hat with the sheer veil. I pinned it in right above the tight bun in my hair. I held my necklace firmly and said, "Supreme, please give me the strength to get through today."

When I got downstairs, the bulletproof limo was waiting for me and two bulletproof trucks were in front and in back of me. Security was of the utmost importance because I didn't want another assassination attempt on my life, especially on the same day I was burying my husband. The promise of seeing Nico die was giving me the strength I needed to get through this. In fact, that was the only reason I had to live.

"Nathan, did you make sure Supreme's parents had bodyguards with them?"

"Yes, I sent Andre and Paul to escort them."

"Good, and the security is extra tight at the church?"

"Yes, we have our own security and Atomic Records has also provided extra protection. The police are also going to be out. They want to make sure it doesn't get out of hand."

We headed toward Queens for the funeral. His parents wanted to have the service at the church Supreme was baptized in. It was only right especially since that was where he was from. When we pulled up to the church it was like reliving the chaos of Biggie's funeral. I remember how Brooklyn was shut down that day with all his fans coming out to show love. At first I wanted a private ceremony but I knew his fans loved him almost as much I did. The news crews swarmed me when I stepped out the car.

"Precious Mills, how do you feel about the death of your husband?" one dizzy-ass reporter asked me.

"Yo, Nathan, get these cameras out my face," I screamed about to punch the bitch in her mouth.

"Everybody out the way," Nathan belted using all 250-pounds of muscle to move the crowd.

When I entered the church, it looked like a hip hop industry convention. Every black rapper, actor and athlete and sprinkles of white associates filled the benches. As I walked toward the front, all eyes were on me. The glares made me hot and I held on to Nathan so I wouldn't pass out. I sat down next to Supreme's parents and his mother was already crying a river. *This is going to be a long memorial service*, I thought to myself.

After the reverend spoke, Supreme's father went to speak, but had to be carried down when he fell out at the podium. I had already made it clear that I wasn't standing up there and saying anything so a few of Supreme's friends and colleagues stood up for him. One of the hardest parts for me was not being able to see his face lying in the coffin. Because of the injuries he sustained his parents and I agreed that Supreme should have a closed coffin. We wanted the world to remember him for how he looked when he was alive, not in death.

"I'm so sorry for your loss," I heard a familiar male voice say from behind me. When I turned around to see his face I was disgusted.

"What are you doing here?" I said with venom in my voice.

I couldn't believe that Pretty Boy Mike had the nerve to show his face at Supreme's funeral. True to form he still had the most perfect, unblemished caramel skin I had ever seen on a man and most women. With his silky jet black hair and long eyelashes you could easily forget how wicked he was.

"Precious, I came to pay my respects. Like everyone else here, I had a lot of admiration for Supreme," Mike said calmly.

"How dare you!" I whispered, not trying to make a scene in the church. "Mike, because of you Rhonda is dead, my unborn child died, and I almost died. Now, you're standing here giving me your condolences when your boy Nico is the reason why Supreme is in that coffin. I don't want your respect or admiration."

"Precious, I know how upset you are, and you have every right to be. But I didn't know Nico was going to kill Rhonda or try to kill you. When he got out, he said all he wanted was to talk to you and find out why you turned on him. He said he finally forgave you and only wanted to wish you the best. Nico misled me, and when I found out about what happened to you and Rhonda I was shocked."

"You're so full of shit. But this isn't the place to discuss this," I said, but before I could complete my thought, we were interrupted.

"I'm sorry to interrupt but hello, Precious." I stared at the tall reddish-skinned man. His eyes told a familiar story but I couldn't place them. I didn't know how I could forget a face so handsome but I kept drawing a blank.

"Hi, do I know you?" I said, still trying to place his face.

"Actually you do. But first I wanted to give you my condolences."

"Thank you. Did you know Supreme well?"

"Actually I only met him a few times when I interned at Atomic Records during the summer. But he was always humble and down-to-earth when he spoke to me. He was a very talented man."

"Yes, he was, but you still haven't told me your name."

"Jamal."

"Jamal Crawford?" I asked in shock. I hadn't seen Jamal in five years. We grew up in the projects of Brooklyn together. But Jamal was always different. He was a bonafide genius. He was also the boy I lost my virginity to.

"Yep, that Jamal," he said with a smile.

"What are you doing here? I didn't know you interned at Atomic Records." Seeing an old friend brought a ray of light to an otherwise dim day.

"How would you? One day you just moved away."

"Aren't you the new president of Atomic Records?" Mike asked, trying to squeeze in the conversation.

"That's me, and you are?" Jamal asked, extending his hand toward Mike.

"Pretty Boy Mike, owner of Pristine Records."

"That's right. I've heard a lot of positive things about you. It's a pleasure to meet you."

"Likewise. I had no idea you were so young. How old are you, nineteen?" Mike said sizing Jamal up.

"Actually, I just celebrated my twenty-first birthday last week," Jamal said, laughing off Mike's dis.

"Wow. You're the president of Atomic Records?" I asked. Jamal was a few months older than me. I couldn't believe that the geeky nerd I used to look at sideways was now running one of the top hip hop labels in the world. Then again, who would've thought I'd be married, better yet alive, at my age.

"Yes, I am. After I graduated college at seventeen," Jamal cut his eyes over at Mike, "I attended Harvard Business School. Each summer and winter break, I interned at Atomic Records. During my last semester the president offered me a job as his apprentice. Then, when he got a more lucrative offer from another label, Atomic's owners asked me to take over. At first everyone was a little reluctant because of my age, but my work ethic speaks for itself."

"I'm not surprised. Congratulations."

"Thank you, Precious. I know you're overwhelmed right now, but in the near future I wanted to sit down and discuss some business regarding Supreme with you. Here's my card. Call me when you feel up to it."

"I will. It was so nice to see you again, Jamal, and thank you for showing your respect for Supreme."

"Of course, it was nice to see you, too," Jamal said before he walked away.

"Seems you have some history with the new president of Atomic Records," Mike said, obviously fishing for information.

"You still haven't excused yourself?" I questioned, wondering what it would take to get Mike out of my space.

"Precious, don't be like that. I care a great deal about you and I want to make sure you're okay."

"You don't even know me and I don't want you to. You're a snake, Mike. Stay away from me."

The whole ride home all I thought about was Jamal. I kept reading his business card over and over again. I knew Jamal would be successful in life and have a great career making a lot of money, but the music business was the last place I thought it would be. He seemed too uptight to be around a bunch of grimy rappers.

He had changed so much. The bifocals were history and his once scrawny body was now well defined with lean muscles. I was looking forward to calling him because I needed to talk to someone from my past. Jamal would understand who Precious Cummings from the projects, not the widow of superstar Supreme, really was.

You Ain't a Killa . . . But I Am

The sound of my cell phone ringing woke me up at eight-thirty a.m. "Hello," I answered with my eyes still closed.

"Yo, Precious I got some info for you." I recognized Smokey's voice and tried to shake myself to wake up.

"What's up?"

"Can you meet me in an hour?"

"Say what you gotta say."

"I don't wanna talk on the phone. This some shit we need to discuss face to face."

"Nico business?"

"No doubt, so can you meet me?"

"Where at?"

"Harlem, at the soul food spot M&G."

"A'ight, give me two hours." It had been a few weeks since I put the hit out on Nico, and I was glad Smokey finally had some information for me.

While taking a shower I debated whether I wanted to bring Nathan and one of my other bodyguards. I knew I needed the protection but at the same time I didn't want them asking questions about my dealings with Smokey. No matter what, I was definitely carrying my heat because there was no telling what was waiting for me in New York.

"Good morning, fellas. I have to run an errand this morning."

"I'll pull the car around," Nathan said.

"Actually, I'll be going alone."

"I don't think that's wise, Precious," he barked.

"Calm down, I got this. If there seems to be a problem you'll be the first person I'll call. But I'm good. I got my girl wit' me." I jumped in the Range because all the other cars were a little too flashy.

When I crossed the George Washington Bridge and hit the Hudson Parkway, I became more anxious, wondering what information Smokey had regarding Nico.

I drove around the block a couple of times before I pulled up in front of the legendary restaurant that was no bigger than my Range but served food as good as hell. I saw Smokey's BMW 525 parked at the curb but he wasn't inside. I figured he was already in the spot but I called his cell to double check. I took out my nine millimeter from the hidden compartment and placed the silencer on the tip of the barrel before placing it in my purse. I hoped that I wouldn't have to use it but you can never be too careful. I slowly walked up in the spot checking in all directions who was in the place. A few couples were seated, getting they grub on and Smokey sat directly facing the door. "What's good, Smokey?"

"Hopefully everything. I think this info I got should put a smile on yo' face."

"Speak," I said, sitting down.

"One of my street informants introduced me to this cat that says he know where Nico is hiding out at."

"Word?"

"Word is born. The nigga wouldn't give me too many details 'cause he want his bread first."

"What details did he give?"

"He said the nigga is staying at some co-op downtown on the West side."

"What? That sounds crazy. You tellin' me that nigga still right here in New York?"

"That's what my man say. Besides, it's not like Nico could have gotten on a plane. Even the feds are looking for him. It makes sense, since he just killed Supreme a few weeks ago."

"How is your informant sure it's Nico?"

"The nigga still hustling. From what I understand he tryna get his paper right before he break out. My informant's cousin sold three diesels to him."

"Nico back selling heroin? Who hitting that nigga off wit' paper?"

"How the story goes, my boy's cousin is a big time hustling nigga. The kingpin nigga sent him to drop off the goods because he got backed up on some other shit. He had no idea Nico was the nigga he was delivering to. Some bitch answered the door and it took Nico a second to come out from the back. He gave him the package and he still wasn't positive it was Nico until he heard the bitch call out his name when he was walking out the door. As far as where he got the paper to buy that shit, I don't know. But I don't think that nigga's cousin be frontin' wit' his diesel so Nico got the cash from somewhere."

"So Nico hauled up wit' some bitch selling diesel? He right under our fuckin' noses."

"Damn right."

"So what's next?"

"The nigga wanna speak to you and make sure that he'll get the bread if he delivers on the body."

"Where he at now?"

"He live right around the corner. I didn't tell him you were coming to meet me but I wanted us to be nearby just in case you was up to seeing him."

"So you believe he on the up-and-up?"

"No doubt. This nigga official. All he want is his paper and Nico is good as dead."

"A'ight, get him on the phone and hook up the meeting."

I sat back and listened to Smokey make the arrangements. Something about the situation was a little suspect, but Smokey sounded so confident with his information. Plus, it was plausible for Nico to be shacking up with some bitch getting his hustle on so he could get the fuck out of New York. Your options are limited when your pockets are empty, so it did make sense. I stored my paranoia in the back of my mind and held on tightly to my purse for backup.

"He ready. I told him we be there in fifteen minutes so he wouldn't know we was just a step away."

"Let's do this. But for your sake this nigga betta be on the up."

Smokey and I small-talked for a few since we had extra time. After I finished my glass of sweet tea, I followed him out the front door. We walked about three blocks until we came to a renovated apartment building in the middle of the projects. It blew my mind how these real estate motherfuckers kept putting all this money into upgrading these apartments, raising the rent so upper-middle-class white people could move in the neighborhood. It didn't matter because niggas still wasn't going anywhere; it would always be the hood. I guess they hoped the local blacks would be wiped out from either drugs or the violence of the streets. They'd be waiting a long time. Niggas had a way to keep multiplying.

"Hold up, this his spot, but let me hit his cell so he'll know we outside," Smokey said as he dialed the number. I stood looking around, feeling the area out. It was the early afternoon and the hood was slowly coming alive.

"Come on, Precious, he live on the second floor." The guy buzzed us in and instead of us taking the elevator I told

Smokey to take the stairs. In a situation like this where I wasn't feeling totally comfortable, I felt I had more room to move taking the stairs if shit was shaky. I was relieved when no niggas had they gats drawn when we reached the floor.

When we got to the door, Smokey knocked and I stood to the side clutching my purse in preparation for anything faulty. Smokey was cool, but I could tell that even though he was in the game and had his ears to the streets, he wasn't no official killer-type nigga. I say that because he was just too relaxed. He knew I was carrying heat and he was strapped, too, but most murder-type niggas always give a quick pat to they piece just to make sure it's right there ready for them to explode on a cat if necessary. Smokey was cheesing as if he was bringing me home for dinner to meet his parents.

After standing for a few seconds, someone finally came and opened the door.

"Wass up?" he said, giving Smokey a pound.

"It's all good, this here is the young lady I was telling you about."

"How you doing? I'm B-Boy." I just politely grinned and nodded my head. Then I zoomed in on his eyes, trying to get a read on him. He looked young, but maybe that was because he had a baby face. He was tall and skinny with a Hershey bar complexion. He had an inviting smile but my gut told me he had another agenda. "Come on in," he said, completely opening the door. Smokey and I stepped inside and to my surprise the apartment was extremely neat and decorated nicely. I figured he must live with his girl because the place definitely had a woman's touch.

"Can I get ya something to drink?"

"Nah, I'm good." I never liked to eat or drink at somebody's crib unless they were my people like that.

"I'll take some soda or something," Smokey said, never being one to turn down nothing that could fill up his belly.

When the guy walked off to the kitchen, I moved closer

to Smokey. "So that the nigga that knows Nico's where-abouts?" I whispered.

"That's him, he seem like good people, right?" he said, nodding his head and grinning. I didn't even respond to Smokey. Instead I studied the room trying to get an indication if anyone else was there. I noticed the window was halfway open and wondered if someone sneaked out not wanting us to see them on our way up.

"Here's your drink, man," B-Boy said, handing a can of Coca-Cola to Smokey. "Ya wanna have a seat?"

"I'm good." I always think better on my feet. Smokey sat down on the couch next to B-Boy.

"A'ight, well, let's get down to it. As I told my man Smokey, I know exactly where Nico is holding court. I have no problem taking that nigga out for the right price, and from what I understand, that price is a million dollars."

"Yeah, you got that price right. You get half up front, half on delivery." I paused for a minute to make B-Boy comfortable like everything was sweet. "So, Nico holed up selling coke that he bought from your cousin? That's how you found out his whereabouts?"

"Yeah, my cousin had me drop off some of that coke and I peeped your man Nico. I remembered my man Smokey telling me there was a hit out on him and I was like this is just my luck."

"You got that right," I said, pulling out my nine and walking toward B-Boy as I put the gun to the side of his head.

"What the fuck is you doing, Precious?" Smokey blurted out and stood up from the couch. I stayed focused with my finger on the trigger as B-Boy sat quietly.

"Smokey, this nigga told you he delivered three packages of heroin to Nico and now he saying coke. That ain't no small oversight, that's a major fuck up." B-Boy slightly bit down on his bottom lip realizing he had messed up. It was good to know Smokey wasn't a part of this farce because by the look on his face he truly didn't see it coming.

"Damn, B-Boy, this was all a set up? Word is born. I thought you was good people."

"Do you even know where Nico is, or was that all part of the scam?" I asked the snake. B-Boy sat there mum. "A'ight, nigga, either you start telling me who you working for or I'm 'bout to put this bullet in you like it ain't nothin'." He was still silent but I caught his eyes glance over by the shut bedroom door.

I put my finger over my mouth indicating to Smokey to be quiet and then signaled for him to come closer to me. Then I whispered, "Pull out your piece. There's somebody in that bedroom; you might have to blast whoever in there," I said, pointing to the closed door.

Smokey got a real shook look on his face before revealing, "Precious, I ain't neva shot nobody before. I ain't no killa."

"Smokey, either kill or be killed. Those are your options. I can't be in two places at one time." As I was talking to Smokey, B-Boy was fidgeting. I knew he was trying to scheme a way to get out this mess. He was also probably wondering why whoever his backup in the bedroom was hadn't come out to save his skinny ass. They were probably sleeping on the job, not knowing B-Boy's cover had been blown.

"Listen here, don't even think about making a move," I said softly but sternly in his ear. "Smokey, you keep this gun to his head and I'll go check the bedroom. If the nigga flinch, lullabye his ass. Now give me your gun." Smokey had a nine like mine, so I would have no problem using it.

Smokey held the gun to B-Boy's head but his nervousness was clear. I just prayed that B-Boy didn't sense it and take advantage of the situation. "If you make a sound, Smokey gonna smoke yo' ass," I said to B-Boy, trying to instill fear. I cautiously walked toward the door, without being in direct range. I stood on the side of the wall and put my right hand on the knob, slowly raising my left arm to firing position. As I was about to open the door, I heard B-Boy scream out.

"Yo, she got a gun!"

Immediately, I fell to the floor and crawled back behind a chair. I looked at Smokey and yelled, "Smoke that nigga!" From the quick glance I got of Smokey, the nigga was frozen. Then the bedroom door flung open and a dude stepped out with his gun raised.

"She over there!" B-Boy screamed out. Before the nigga could turn around in my direction I stood up behind the chair and blasted off three shots. Two hit him in the chest and one in the neck. Both Smokey and B-Boy looked with their mouths wide open as his body fell to the floor. "Bitch, you killed my brother!"

With Smokey still not making no moves, B-Boy used the opportunity to wrestle the gun out of his hand, but I ended all that. I was a few feet away but my aim was crazy, and my shot put a bullet in the back of B-Boy's head. His head exploded and blood splattered in Smokey's face. He bent over for a minute and I thought the nigga was going to vomit. I ran in the kitchen, grabbed a towel and ran some water on it. "Smokey, wipe your face off," I said, handing him the towel.

"Precious, you just killed two niggas. I-I-I ain't neva se-se-seen no shit like that before. Where the fuck you learned tha-that shit?" The nervousness in his voice had Smokey stuttering.

"The streets, but baby boy we ain't got time to talk about all that. We need to get the fuck outta here. I know somebody called the police by now. Let's go." I slowly opened the door to see if it was safe in the hallway and to my despair I saw two dudes coming around the corner running toward the apartment. Hurriedly, I shut and locked the door.

"What's wrong?" Smokey asked, sounding like a scared bitch.

"Yo, some niggas is coming, and my bet is they coming for us." Instantly, I remembered the open window. Since we were on the second floor, the jump down wouldn't be bad. I ran toward the window and kicked out the screen. When I looked down, there was a big garbage dumpster underneath.

"I know you ain't 'bout to jump out that window?"

"No, *we* are about to jump out this window. Unless you wanna wait here for them niggas to kick down the door." If Smokey knew how to handle his heat I would've waited and shut them niggas down. But I knew there were at least two dudes behind that door, maybe more. I didn't know what type of artillery they were working with so the risk was just too great. "So what you doing, you coming wit' me or staying here?" When Smokey heard the shots now being fired through the door he ran toward the window.

"Let's do this before I change my mind."

"You go first, just in case they bust through the door before I jump. I can at least fire shots to protect myself."

"You sure?" he asked, knowing his scared ass wanted to be first anyway.

"Yeah, nigga, now hurry the fuck up," I barked, about to push Smokey out the window. The minute he landed in the trash, the door flew open. I didn't even have time to wait until Smokey got out the dumpster. I just jumped and landed right on top of his head. We both struggled to get out as one of the dudes started busting off sparks at us.

"What have I got myself into?" Smokey questioned as we fell out the garbage.

"We ain't got time for questions, hand me my gun." I needed both weapons because if those niggas came at us I needed to blast simultaneously. Smokey handed me my nine and we sprinted toward the only way out. When we got to the corner some dude was jumping off the stairs to the front entrance of the building. By the quickness of his moves I knew he was coming for us. I grabbed Smokey's arm. "This way!" We began hauling ass and I couldn't believe I was running down the street in broad daylight with a gun in each hand. Luckily we were on a side street and no one was really out. When I looked back to see if the enemy was still on our tail I saw Smokey bent over in the middle of the block trying to catch his breath. I knew the nigga was out of shape but damn, this was the wrong time for this shit. "Come on, Smokey!" I screamed out.

"Precious, give me a minute. Word is born, I'm tired as a motherfucker. I think we lost the cat anyway." The minute those words left Smokey's mouth I saw the enemy coming up on him like a quiet storm.

"Come on, Smokey, move it, that nigga behind you!" I yelled as I ran toward him with guns aimed, ready to fire. But I was too late. The enemy discharged about five shots in Smokey's back. His body fell over on the cement. By the time he put the last bullet in Smokey, I was close enough to start blasting off and just lit the nigga up. I checked Smokey's pulse, hoping there was still a chance he was alive. But it was over for him. "I'm sorry, Smokey," I said before dashing back down the street headed for my escape.

Deadly Infatuation

Lying back in the marble Jacuzzi, I tried to relax after the chaotic events from earlier in the day. The French vanilla scented candles surrounding the tub and the second glass of wine I was drinking helped to unwind my body but did little to erase the memory of the bloodshed. To make matters worse, I was no closer to finding out where Nico was, and I had no answers as to who those niggas were working for. Something told me they were playing this game for somebody else and I needed to know who.

Now that Smokey was dead I had to find another connect to get my street information from. "Damn, Smokey is dead," I mumbled out loud. I felt some kinda way about that. I was riddled with guilt for bringing Smokey in some shit that he couldn't handle. Yes, he was a willing participant but he had no idea the stakes were so high. The streets were deadlier than ever for me, because I didn't know who was who or what was what. Everybody had an agenda, including me.

When I stepped out the tub I heard knocking at my bedroom door. I grabbed my robe to see who it was. "Precious, it's me, Nathan, I have your car keys." After the shoot out in Harlem, instead of going back to get my Range I took a taxi home. Hell, I didn't know if them niggas knew what type of whip I was in. They could've been on a stake out. When I arrived home I sent Nathan to go pick up my car.

"Thanks so much," I said, taking my keys from him.

"No problem. But Precious, what happened today? You came home looking distraught. Why was you over in Harlem anyway?"

"Damn, you asking a lot of questions."

"I'm just concerned. Supreme would want me to look out for you and my gut is telling me you involved in some heavy shit."

"I appreciate your concern, Nathan, but I'm good. If I need you I will let you know." I shut the door and sat on my bed. Supreme had a lot of love for Nathan but I didn't trust him with my personal business. He had never done anything to me, but it was a known code of the street not to trust anyone, especially people who claimed to care about your well-being.

The next day, I didn't wake up until two o'clock in the afternoon. My body needed the rest. It had been non-stop action since I was discharged from the hospital. I honestly wanted to get away from everything. Recouping on some faraway island was what I craved, but Nico was what I hungered for. I wouldn't be able to enjoy anything until that nigga was dead. As crazy as it might sound, I wasn't even mad at Nico for trying to kill me. I knew after I got him locked up, it would never be safe for both of us to walk the same streets. But I underestimated Nico. I thought he'd be spending the rest of his life behind bars. Now that he was free, taking me out was a given and I wouldn't expect anything less from him. But killing Supreme was unforgivable. This was between me and Nico. He took away the only man who ever truly loved me. When Supreme died, so did all my dreams.

After getting dressed I went downstairs, starving for something to eat.

"Hi, Anna. I know it's the middle of the afternoon, but can you make me some breakfast?"

"Of course, Mrs. Mills."

"Where are today's papers?"

"I'll get them for you. You also have a message from a Mr. Jamal Crawford." I had been meaning to call Jamal, but of course there had been nothing but drama the last few weeks. *I'm going to call him the minute I finish eating breakfast,* I thought to myself.

First thing I did when I got the *"New York Post"* in my hands was turn to the crime section. Sure enough, the newspaper had a small article about my incident the day before titled, "A Bloody Massacre in Harlem." Of course the police had no witnesses; even if someone did see something, no one was talking. The streets always be watching but rarely ever talk unless there are young children involved. No one in the hood wanted the blood of innocent little ones on their hands.

I wanted to make sure Smokey had a proper burial and that his immediate family was financially straight, but I didn't know any of his people. He mentioned he had a daughter but that's all I knew. I didn't want to go around asking too many questions because no one could know I was dead in the center of the "Bloody Massacre." Three of those bodies were mine. I would figure something out.

After devouring the French toast and home fries Anna cooked I took my glass of mimosa and went outside to call Jamal.

"Jamal Crawford's office, how may I help you?" his receptionist greeted me. A smile crept across my face when I heard that. Jamal had done real good for himself. I never doubted he wouldn't, but to actually see it come to fruition was amazing.

"Yes, this is Precious Mills returning his call."

"Hi, Mrs. Mills, he was expecting your call, let me put you through." There was a slight pause and then Jamal picked up.

"Hi, Precious, thanks for getting back to me."

"I meant to call you a while ago, but with everything that's been going on, it was hectic."

"I understand. I should've given you more time before I called but there were some business matters that really couldn't wait. I spoke to Supreme's attorney and he said you're in charge of his estate, so I need your clearance for a few things."

"That's not a problem. Just let me know how I can help."

"It would be great if you could squeeze me in for lunch or dinner in the next couple of days so we can go over some paperwork."

"No problem, how about tomorrow night?"

"Great, I'll make dinner reservations at Cipriani for seven, is that good for you?"

"Actually, if you don't mind can we have dinner here at my house? I can have Anna prepare a lovely meal. I'm just not up for going out in public yet."

"I'm so sorry. How insensitive of me. I would love to come over for dinner. Is the same time alright?"

"Of course, is there anything in particular you want Anna to cook?"

"A good steak is always nice."

"Then steak it is. I'll see you tomorrow. Bye, Jamal."

I was looking forward to dinner with Jamal. Even when we were in high school I always felt as if I could trust him. Something about him seemed so honorable, which was rare coming from the grimy Brooklyn projects we grew up in. I needed a confidant, and I hoped Jamal could be it. As I continued to think about Jamal my cell rang and the call was from a 917 number that I didn't recognize. At first I wasn't going to answer it but then I said, "Fuck it." I heard loud music in the background when I answered the phone.

"Hello," someone mumbled, but the music was so loud I couldn't hear shit.

"I can't hear you!" I screamed over the phone so whoever was calling me could either hang up and try back later or go to a less noisy area and speak the fuck up.

"My bad, is this better now?" a familiar-sounding male voice asked.

"Yeah, who is this?"

"It's me, Mike. Please don't hang up the phone, Precious."

"Mike, what do you want and how did you get my cell number?"

"To answer your first question, I want to see you. Precious, we need to talk."

"We ain't got nothin' to talk about."

"It's about Nico. I have some information that I believe will be helpful to you."

"Now why would you want to help me? I thought Nico was your friend, or does a snake like you have no friends?"

"Precious, there is no need for the venom. Like I told you at the funeral, I had no idea what Nico was up to. The streets and I are very disappointed with his actions. Supreme was a legend in this industry. He will be sorely missed."

"Oh, it was fucked up for him to take out Supreme but it was okay for him to try and have me wiped off the face of this earth?"

"I'm not saying that Precious, but the Supreme ordeal came from nowhere. So, can we meet somewhere and talk? I promise what I have to say is of great importance."

"Then say it now."

"I don't disclose pertinent information over the phone."

"I'll tell you what, Mike. Since my first priority is to have my husband's killer brought to justice then I'll allow you ten minutes of my time. But you'll have to come to my home alone, and of course my bodyguards will search you. So don't come armed or you won't make it past the gate. You can come tomorrow evening at six. Don't be late." I hung up the phone dreading seeing Mike. I would handle my business with him before my dinner with Jamal. Mike was a snake but he might be the link I needed to bring down Nico. Only time would tell.

I spent the rest of my day trying to decide what questions to ask Mike. I knew he had a lot of street connections and more than likely had an idea of Nico's whereabouts. Still, I had to be careful with my approach. He might be some big time music mogul now, but just like me, the hood ran through his blood. If I played my cards right, Mike could be an endless pool of information. If I came at him wrong, I wouldn't get shit.

That evening when I went to bed I tossed and turned the entire night. My mind was flooded with questions regarding Nico and my body yearned to be held by Supreme. The two of them had been the most important men in my life, so it only seemed logical that at every moment of each day one of them was on my mind.

Ring…ring…

"Hello," I said looking at my clock. It wasn't even eight o'clock in the morning. Who could be calling me this early?

"Good morning, Precious. I was calling to confirm our meeting for this evening at six."

"You can't be serious. You're interrupting my sleep to confirm some fuckin' meeting? You're taking this music industry shit way too serious."

"It's not about the music industry; it's about handling my business. I have business with you and I want to make sure that it's still on. My schedule is always full and if for some reason you've chosen to cancel, I need to know so I can make room for someone else."

"That won't be necessary. Our meeting is still on. I'll see you at six." I flipped my cell phone closed, slightly frustrated. Since the first time I met Mike, I couldn't quite figure him out. There was no doubt he was extremely smart, but there was something else. Since calling and confirming meetings seemed to be the thing to do, I put a call in to Jamal.

"Hi, can I speak to Jamal Crawford?"

"Who's calling?"

"This is Precious Mills."

"Hold on, Mrs. Mills." For the few seconds Jamal's assistant had me on hold I glanced at my hands and feet and realized that a pedicure and manicure were calling my name. The next call I would be making was for an in-house appointment.

"I hope you're not calling to cancel?" Jamal said when he picked up his phone.

"No, actually I was calling to confirm."

"Wow, that's funny. I was going to make the same call to you, but I thought you were still sleeping."

"I'll admit I'm no early bird. Someone woke me up, and you know once that happens there is no way you can go back to sleep," I said with a slight laugh.

"I understand. So we're still on for seven?"

"No doubt."

"Great, so I'll see you then." Jamal was like a different person now. His voice was so confident. No one would ever believe that he used to be a certified ghetto nerd.

The day flew by. After having a conference call with my attorney for over an hour and then sitting through my pedicure and manicure, it was time to get dressed for my first meeting of the evening. My appearance had to be on point because a woman's looks meant everything. You had a much better chance of making a man jump through hoops for a pretty face than a busted one. But just a pretty face wasn't enough for me. I liked to get a nigga's dick hard off the first glance. That way they would be so busy trying to calm down their third leg that they wouldn't be able to focus and have their guard up when I was picking their brain for information.

I decided to slip on a banging-ass red number for the evening. The one-piece Chloé jersey jumpsuit hugged my body perfectly and made my now slimmed-down figure voluptuous in the right spots.

"Precious, your guest has arrived." By the sound of Nathan's voice, I knew he detested seeing Mike come through the front door. Mike's friends were responsible for busting a champagne bottle over his head. It was a long time ago, but I guess you never get over something like that.

I looked myself over one last time before heading out. I stood at the top of the grand staircase. Mike gazed up at me from where he stood in the marble foyer. It was like that scene from "*Scarface*"—the first time Tony Montana laid eyes on Elvira with nothing but lust in his eyes.

"I see that you're right on time," I said, slowly walking down the stairs.

"Promptness is a must in my book."

"Follow me." I led Mike into the den. Nathan and one of my other bodyguards were behind us. When I closed the door they stood post right outside. They knew he was unarmed but hands could be just as deadly. "I have another meeting very shortly so let's get right to it. What information do you have for me?"

"Relax for a minute. You obviously had more than business on your mind when you decided to put on that outfit."

"Excuse me?"

"You heard me. Any man would get a hard-on looking at that number, but I suppose that was the objective. Well, let me applaud you," he said, clapping his hands.

"I don't find your behavior amusing."

"That's too bad, because I find yours to be. Let's get one

thing out the way. I'll be the first to admit that you're proba-bly the sexiest, most beautiful woman I've ever seen in my life. But your beauty is only going to move me so far. It'll never blind me to the point that I lose control over a situa-tion, like I'm sure it has with other men in your life."

"Save the bullshit. You're the one who asked to come see me, let's not forget that. So my appearance needs to be an afterthought, not your first one." I knew my voice had a tone of irritation in it and I had to calm myself down. Mike had a way of getting under my skin but I couldn't let him know that, although he probably already did. The smug son-of-a-bitch had the nerve to read me. His assessment was correct, but didn't anybody ask him.

"Enough of this small talk; let's discuss what I came to see you about."

"My point exactly." I had to say that so Mike wouldn't think he was running this show.

"I don't know if you heard about this, but there was a major shootout in Harlem the other day. From what my street informants told me it was because of some million dollar ransom you put out on Nico." I damn near dropped the glass of cognac I just poured myself. Luckily my back was turned away from Mike so he couldn't see the stunned look on my face.

"Million dollar ransom? You need to check your so-called informants because they digging up bad dirt. I'm letting the police handle the investigation of Supreme's murder."

"Then I guess that means you have no interest in know-ing who was behind the set-up. Since that's the case, then my business here is done." Mike turned to walk away and I couldn't stop myself, I wanted to know.

"Who was behind it?" Mike stopped for a moment, with his back toward me. I imagined him grinning at me caving in, and it made my skin crawl.

"Nico. He got word about your hit and came up with a plan

of his own."

"What, to have me killed?"

"I'm sure that's what he intended the end result to be, but Nico planned on walking away with the money first. From what I understand, B-Boy's cousin not only has a business relationship with Nico but a personal one. They came up hustling together. So when B-Boy told his cousin about the hit that was lingering over Nico's head, he warned Nico. Nico figured B-Boy could pose as the hit man for hire. Let you pay him the first half up front, and then take some fake photos with Nico dead and get part two. It wasn't a bad plan but somehow B-Boy fucked up and he ended up dead along with his brother and one of his partners. Oh, and so did your middle man," he added. "I believe his name was Smokey." Mike paused before continuing. "Answer me this, Precious, were you the one responsible for the dead bodies in Harlem?" he asked, mocking me slightly.

"You seem to have it all figured out. You should be telling me the answer to that question."

"Then I say, yes, except for Smokey of course."

"Sorry, I can't take credit for ending the lives of those bitch-ass niggas. But whoever left them flat-lining did a commendable service for the community."

"That's too bad. Word on the streets is that a woman who is not only gorgeous but mean with the heat is responsible for the havoc up top. They speak of her as if she's some sort of female superhero. From the description I just knew it had to be you. I was wrong. You're not the baddest bitch in New York after all." I gave Mike a smirk of disgust. The head games he was trying to play with me had now gone beyond just being annoying.

"Listen, the real question is, do you know the whereabouts of Nico? And if you did, would you tell me?" Mike walked back and forth a few times as if in deep thought. His tailored dark navy ensemble moved with each movement of his body. I always heard that real gangsters wear suits and watching Mike draped in his was only authenticating the statement.

"You may not believe this, but I don't know where Nico is hiding out. The last time I saw him was right after he shot you."

"You saw Nico then? What did he say?" This was the first time I had spoken to anybody who had a first-hand account of not only seeing Nico, but talking to him. My whole body filled with the anticipation of knowing what he discussed with Mike.

"He called me right after the shooting and we met at the Pier. He told me what happened and that Supreme and his bodyguards witnessed what went down. That had him on edge, because he knew he would be wanted for murder. He had just beat one murder rap and was free again only to turn around and get charged with another. But of course at that time, unbeknownst to us, like the cat you are, you survived with eight lives still intact."

"What else did he say when you saw him?"

"He asked me for some money so he could get out of town. I had no time to head to the bank so I could only come up with a hundred thousand. He took it and I wished him well."

"So that's how he was able to buy that diesel from B-Boy's cousin, the money you hit him off wit'. You're responsible for funding his madness."

"Precious, when I gave Nico that money, I thought you were dead. Never did I believe Nico would come back to finish you off and kill Supreme in the process. Nico told me he was leaving town. Giving him a hundred thousand was the least I could do for him. As I told you, me and Nico go way back."

"Yeah, it seems Nico goes way back wit' a lot of people."

"I told you in the studio a long time ago, Nico is a true

kingpin just like me. He will always have powerful people looking out for him."

"So if Nico called you tomorrow, would you go and help him knowing that he is responsible for Supreme's death?"

"No, I wouldn't. But not because of Supreme, but because of you," Mike said, now standing right in front of me. He put his hand under my chin and tilted my face up so my eyes were locked with his. *Pretty Boy Mike*, I thought to myself. *Now I know why this nigga makes me so frustrated— I'm attracted to this son-of-a-bitch, always have been. And I hate myself for it.*

"Because of me? Why?" I questioned, trying to shake my feelings. His hand was still grasping my chin and I felt like I was being hypnotized by the penetration of his eyes. Maybe Mike was right. True kingpins are different. They got this certain darkness in their eyes. Nico had it and so did he. That darkness always drew me in. It was like it called my name. Just then, I heard Nathan knocking at the door.

Saved by the bell. "Precious, Jamal Crawford is here to see you."

"Show him to the living room, I'll be right there." I couldn't believe that an hour had gone by already. I only planned to spend fifteen minutes with Mike but now I wished I had an hour more.

"What is Jamal Crawford here to see you about?" he asked, taking his hand away from my face.

"We have some business to discuss regarding Supreme." The way I answered Mike's question so quickly, I knew I was in trouble. Somehow this slick-ass nigga managed to get next to me. I didn't want to believe it, but Mike had me infatuated.

"What type of business, if you don't mind me asking?"

"Before Supreme died he had a lot of music recorded and I own the rights so Jamal wants to make me an offer on behalf of Atomic Records."

"How much is he offering?"

"That's what he's here to discuss."

"Before you sign anything with Atomic make sure you let me take a look."

"They have lawyers for that, and why would you want to take a look?"

"I don't want you to get cheated and I know this business inside and out. That music is worth a fortune, especially now that Supreme is dead. I'm just looking out for your best interest." I gave Mike a slight smile, assuming that his kind gesture was more of an attempt to score brownie points than him actually caring about what deal I struck with Atomic Records.

"Thank you, I'll definitely keep that in mind before I sign on the dotted line."

"That's all I ask. Well, I won't keep you." Mike headed toward the door and I honestly didn't want him to leave.

"Wait, you never told me why?"

"Why, what?"

"Because of me, you said you would no longer help Nico. Why?"

"I'll have to answer that over dinner." Nathan was right there waiting by the door when Mike opened it. He was more than happy to show him out. I guzzled down the glass of cognac that had been waiting for me since Mike's arrival. The slight burning sensation that hit my chest as the liquor went down my throat gave me a burst of energy. I tossed my head back and sauntered out the den ready for part two with Jamal.

When I entered the living room Jamal was sitting on the elongated couch with a bottle of wine in his hand. "Is that for me?"

Jamal initially gave me a look as if he didn't know what I was talking about, until I motioned my eyes to the bottle. "Yes, it's for us. I thought we could drink it over dinner. I hope you like red wine."

"I'm more of a champagne or dark liquor kinda girl, but I'm up for trying something new. I'll pour us a glass." Jamal handed me the bottle and I went into the kitchen where Anna was preparing dinner.

"Anna, my guest has arrived. So whenever you're ready you can serve dinner."

"Yes, Mrs. Mills." As I poured the wine, I still couldn't get Mike off my mind. His personality was a combination of Nico and Supreme. Maybe that's what I found so appealing. Nevertheless, Mike was trouble and someone I needed to stay far away from, especially since I couldn't deny my attraction to him.

When I went back into the living room, Jamal was looking through me and Supreme's wedding album. I almost dropped the wine glasses due to shock. I hadn't been in the living room since I was shot and had forgotten all about those pictures. Seeing Jamal sitting there with the book in his hand brought all these emotions to the surface.

"I didn't mean to intrude," Jamal said at he noticed I was standing before him frozen.

"No, it's fine. I just haven't seen that book in so long."

"You were a beautiful bride."

"Thank you. That was the happiest day of my life. Now it's just a memory that causes me pain."

"I'm so sorry, but I know that doesn't help. I can't begin to say that I feel your pain."

"Yeah, I wouldn't wish losing the love of your life on anyone. It's kinda bizarre. Who would've ever thought that Precious Cummings from the Brooklyn projects would be talking about losing the love of her life? Not only that, but the love being superstar rapper Supreme. One better, is that I'm talking about it with you. My childhood neighbor and the man I lost my virginity to."

"It is a bit awkward. You never know what direction life will lead you in. But it's not surprising to me that you ended up marrying a man like Supreme. Every man that laid eyes on you fell in love, including me."

"Jamal, we were kids. What you felt for me was puppy love, nothing more."

"It didn't feel that way then. I was crushed when you stopped coming to see me."

"You knew it was only temporary. I was very honest with you," I said with a teasing smile.

"I know. You wanted to practice how to better your sex skills, so you could blow the mind of some big time hustler."

"Hearing you say that now sounds crazy."

"Those were your words, not mine."

"I know. So much has changed since then."

"After you left the projects I never saw you again. I would overhear conversations and people would say you were the wife of the infamous Nico Carter. That he treated you like a queen. You became a legend in Brooklyn. After your mother died I went to her funeral and I hoped to see you there. I saw your mother a few times before her death and she had changed her life around. No one could believe how beautiful she looked, just like her daughter," Jamal said solemnly. "That's why it was so tragic when she was murdered."

I nodded my head, fighting back the tears that were welling in my eyes. "It seems that everyone that I've ever loved has been taken away from me. But you know what the worst part is?" I stated, staring directly into Jamal's eyes. "In each of their deaths I'm somehow responsible."

"You can't blame yourself for the madness of the streets. You're just as innocent as the victims themselves."

"Jamal, there is nothing innocent about me." Jamal had no idea that he was about to break bread with a killer. He still remembered me as Precious Cummings, the girl everyone felt sorry for because her mother was a crack whore. Oh, how things had changed.

"You'll always be innocent in my eyes." I could hear the sincerity in Jamal's voice. It was rather touching.

"Enough about me, look at you. *You* really have changed."

"You're right about that. Who would've believed I'd be the president of a hip hop label?"

"Me. Maybe not hip hop, but the president of a company—yes," I said honestly. "I knew you could rule the world if you wanted. You were just that smart."

"That means a lot coming from you," he said. I wanted to get off the subject of me, because for some reason I felt guilty about how I treated Jamal a few years back. Yeah, we were only kids but I was feeling like maybe I took advantage of him in some ways.

"Did you know Rhonda? She worked at Atomic."

"I didn't know her well, was she a friend of yours?"

"Yes. We were very close. She was actually my roommate before I married Supreme."

"Really, we worked in different departments, but we talked occasionally. Everyone was in shock when she was murdered."

"Yeah, so was I. Another death I'm responsible for," I mumbled under my breath.

"Mrs. Mills, your dinner is ready."

"Thank you, Anna. Let's eat." Jamal followed me to the dining room and we devoured the delicious steak Anna prepared. Being around Jamal was so easy. I didn't feel as if I had to put my guard up as I would with everyone else. His behavior seemed genuine, without any ulterior motive.

"Dinner was delicious. We've spent so much time playing catch up that I almost forgot the reason I scheduled this dinner in the first place."

"That's right, there was a reason. You have Supreme business to discuss."

Jamal gave me a charming smile right before he cut to the chase. "Unlike many artists, Supreme fulfilled his record contract. He put out a CD every year, sometimes two. Right before his death he was in negotiations with Atomic Records to sign a new multi-million dollar deal."

"I guess that's impossible now that he is dead?" I inquired.

"Actually, it's not."

"I don't understand."

"You know how much Supreme loved being in the studio. He completed enough new tracks to come out with three full CDs. Technically he owns them. They were done on his own time and money after he fulfilled his obligations with Atomic. He let us listen to most of the tracks during negotiations, and it's his best work. That work is part of his estate so you now own his music. Atomic Records wants to buy that from you."

"Really, for how much?"

"I'm not going to bullshit you, Precious, his music is worth a lot, especially now that he's dead. Supreme had the same type of fan following as someone like Tupac. I believe you should sit down with your attorney and discuss what type of numbers you should be asking for."

"I appreciate you being so honest with me. You could've thrown a price out, and if it sounded right I probably would've taken it, no questions asked. I mean, what the hell do I know about the music business? Plus, Supreme made so many lucrative investments I have more money than I could possibly spend in this lifetime or the next."

"Well, maybe it's time you get familiar with it. Supreme has left you a very rich woman. You need to make your decisions wisely."

"Thanks for the advice. I'll definitely keep that in mind. Maybe you can come back over again soon, and we can discuss further."

Jamal paused before saying with grin, "I don't think my fiancée would like that too much. She would take one look at you and shut that down."

"Fiancée, you're getting married?"

"Yes, I am, in a few months."

"Congratulations. She's a lucky woman. Look at you. You're this handsome, successful business man."

"Thank you, but I feel like the lucky one. Nina is a terrific woman. I think you would like her, Precious."

"I'm sure I would. Maybe one day you two can come over for dinner."

"That's an excellent idea. But let's do one better. This time you can come over to my place for dinner. I'll set that up with Nina and give you a call."

"Definitely. I'll also speak to my attorney and get back to you with a price."

"Great. I look forward to seeing you again. Have a good night."

"You too." I felt some kinda way when Jamal revealed he was engaged, almost jealous. Maybe it was because I felt he was about to embark on the life that I was supposed to share with Supreme. Whatever it was, I had to admit it made me curious. I was interested in meeting the woman who had stolen my first's heart. Besides, letting Jamal and his fiancée play host and getting Supreme's business in order would keep my mind occupied and hopefully dispel my potentially deadly infatuation with Pretty Boy Mike.

Never Say Never

For the next few weeks, I kept going back and forth with my attorney regarding what type of money Atomic Records should be bringing to the table, and if I should shop to other places in order to start a bidding war for Supreme's music. Between that, I avoided Mike's calls because I hadn't quite figured out how to deal with our undeniable attraction. I did need him as a source of information to see if he heard about any moves Nico was making, but I wasn't sure I could trust the feedback. Mike wasn't the type of man that could be handled with kid gloves, and until I determined how to make him work for me and not against me, I decided to keep him at arm's length.

Later on that day, I had a doctor's appointment in Midtown. I scheduled a meeting with a top-notch plastic surgeon to have reconstructive surgery done on the scar left on my chest from the bullet, courtesy of Nico. The physician who made the original incision did an excellent job, but why not make it less noticeable if possible? After my consultation and setting up the actual date for the surgery I decided to stop off at my favorite Dominican chicken and rice spot in Washington Heights. I double-parked and flicked on my hazard lights before running in the joint. After about five minutes they handed me my order, and when I walked out the door this dude smacked right into me. "Excuse me, ma, I'm so sorry," he said, picking up the bag of food he caused me to drop.

"Damn, is my food straight?"

"Yeah, luckily it's tightly sealed. Ain't nothin' come out of place." The stranger handed me back my bag and apologized again before going in the Dominican spot. I was just relieved I didn't have to go back inside and stand in that line again.

"Shit, some stupid motherfucker blocking me in. Now I gotta wait for the person to come back so I can pull out this bitch," I vented out loud. I sat in my car, rolled down the window and listened to my Nas mixed CD. Five minutes later the same dude that bumped into me came out of the restaurant and approached the car blocking me in—he was the driver.

"Damn, ma, you must be sick of me. First the food, now I'm holding you up. My fault." *Whatever nigga,* I thought to myself, *just move yo' shit.*

"No problem," I lied. After the stranger moved his car, I pulled off, and before long I was on the George Washington Bridge heading back to Jersey. By the time I got on Route 17 North heading toward Saddle River, the normally smooth ride in my Benz was feeling rather shaky. Part of me wanted to keep going but another part of me didn't want to take any chances. It was getting dark, and I had to go up those long winding roads to get to the estate. I reasoned it was better to get off and stop at a gas station to have my tires checked. I got off at the first exit that had a gas station. The sign indicated it was two miles away but because I was being cautious and driving slowly it seemed like twenty miles.

"What the fuck!" I screamed when out the blue, a car smashed me from behind. I was so busy looking at the signs that I hadn't noticed a car was even behind me. For the first time I was regretting that I had even allowed myself to drive today. Nathan begged me to use the driver but being the independent bitch that I am, I wanted to drive myself. Now here I was in the middle of a dark-ass road with a fucked up tire and some silly fuck who just hit the back of my car.

I saw a man step out his car but because it was now dark and there were no street lights, I couldn't get a clear view of his face. I started to reach for the glove compartment to get my gun because the situation was feeling all wrong to me. But it was too late. When our eyes locked I realized it was the same dude that bumped into me at the Dominican restaurant. He gave me the most sinister grin as he used a hammer to bust open my window. I turned my body toward the passenger seat as the glass shattered.

"Bitch, where you think yo' ass goin'?" he said, grabbing my hair. He held my hair in a firm grip as he pushed my entire body to the passenger side and he sat in the driver's seat. He slammed the door and tossed down the hammer and pulled out a huge sharp knife.

"What the fuck, you tryna rob me? You followed me all the way from the Heights for some money? If that's what you after, I'll get you money, but you need to put that fuckin' knife away."

"Bitch, you about to die, and still poppin' all that shit."

"Die, what the fuck you wanna kill me for? I don't even know you." My mind was spinning, wondering if this was some beef haunting me from the past.

"Yeah, but you knew my cousins."

"Yo' cousins, who the fuck is yo' cousins?"

"You don't remember when you shot B-Boy and his brother? Them my cousins. You a trife bitch. First you try to take down Nico, and then you kill my people."

"I don't know what the fuck you talkin' 'bout, you got the wrong bitch." At this moment all I was trying to do was buy time. The nigga had a knife to my neck, but I had my girl in the glove compartment. I had been in enough jams to know that it's the one who moves the fastest that lives the longest. Right now he had the upper hand.

"Don't try that slick shit wit' me. I know who the fuck you is. But yo' death ain't gonna be quick like theirs. Nah, no guns, baby girl, I got this knife so I can slice you up real nice. Pretty soon you'll be able to join your dead husband in hell. But before that, I'm gonna enjoy torturing you. You see that road off to the side? We're going to park the car over there so people can't see us from this here street."

"Then what?" I questioned, keeping him running off at the mouth as I plotted my next move.

"I'm going to tie you up and toss yo' ass in the trunk of my car. Take you to a special place where I can fuck you up and no one can hear your screams." I knew I had to act fast. Once my hands were tied up it was a wrap. On the floor under me, I eyed my alligator purse with the steel clasp sitting on top of my bag of food. It was a long shot, but if I was going to die I would go out fighting. The only advantage I had was that he believed I was unarmed and that he was the only one with access to a weapon. Because of that he would be a little bit more lax.

"That's fucked up. So your plan is to torture and then kill me. I never intended to kill your cousins. The whole situation just got out of hand. I'm sure we can work this out." I was keeping the conversation flowing as my mind was preparing for the great escape.

"You being awfully calm for a bitch that's about to get it, but we wasting time here sitting and talking 'bout this shit." The dude was becoming animated with his hands as I got him talking more.

"Well, I guess we betta break out, so you can get this shit over wit'," I said, moving my head back so the knife wouldn't be directly under my neck.

"I guess so." The nigga still had a firm grip on my hair but for a brief moment he relaxed the hand that was holding the knife. I knew it was now or never. With great quickness I bent my head down and bit as hard as I could into the flesh of his hand. The pain was so excruciating that he let go of the knife. I couldn't see where the knife fell, so with one hand I grabbed my purse with the steel side upward and bashed it over the dude's mouth. The skin above his lip opened and blood started squirting out from the gash. With the pain from his hand and now his face growing stronger, he let go of my hair to stop the blood. By this time I reached inside the glove compartment to retrieve my gun.

"You bitch, I'ma kill you." The dude reached down to get his hammer.

"Not tonight, motherfucker," I said as I cocked my nine and sparked off two shots. One hit the side of his face the other went through his neck. Blood was everywhere. I looked around as I got out the car and walked to the driver's side. I opened the door and pushed the nigga's body to the passenger side. Luckily he was an average-sized dude, so I was able to maneuver him. I then drove up to that same side street where he planned to tie me up. I had to focus. No way was I going to get the cops involved with this, but I had to get rid of this nigga's body. From him scratching my face and pulling my hair, my DNA was all over his body. There was no way I could leave the dude on the side of the road. Shit, I watched "CSI"—they were no joke. He had to be disposed of permanently. But I would need the help of a man for a job of this magnitude.

At first I considered calling Nathan, but that was a no go. He seemed loyal but he was also legal. He wasn't no street nigga that knew how to dump bodies and shit like that. He would no doubt want me to notify the police which wasn't even negotiable. I only knew of one person I could call who would know how to make this problem go away. I'd owe him, but my back was against the wall. I located my purse and got my cell phone. I slowly dialed his number, hoping that another person that could help would pop in my mind, but I knew there was no one else. "I need you."

Forty-five minutes later a silver Aston Martin pulled up behind me. I jumped out, actually relieved help had arrived. "It must be killing you that you had to call me, huh?"

"Mike, ask me questions later. Right now we have to get rid of this body and my car."

"The car I saw on the side of the road, is it the dead man's?"

"Yes."

"All your paperwork and whatever else you need, take it out your car. After we leave, two of my men are coming to take the vehicles and dispose of the body."

"So what, we're leaving?"

"Of course, I have trained professionals that know how to handle this. Just go get your belongings. I'll meet you in my car." I hated turning to Mike for help, but he was the man I needed. I went through the car and trunk three times, making sure I didn't leave a thing. Before I left, I went through the dude's pockets and took his wallet. When I was alone I would go through it and find out his name and if anything led to Nico's location.

"Ok, I'm ready." Hesitantly, I jumped into Mike's car.

After five minutes of driving, Mike finally broke the silence. "Are you ready to tell me what happened?"

"Not really, but I guess I do owe you an explanation."

"Without a doubt, especially since I'm the last person I thought you'd call to get out a jam. But then again this isn't no ordinary situation."

"No, it's not. The long and the short of it, that dead nigga is B-Boy's cousin. He followed me from the Heights, or maybe from before that. His slick ass probably fucked wit' my tire, too. Don't mind me, I'm just thinking out loud here.

But anyway, when I pulled off the highway he slammed his car into me. Next thing I know this nigga got a knife to my throat telling me how he gonna torture and slice me up. Of course he didn't know that I had my bitch wit' me, and I was able to turn the tables and light that nigga up."

"Precious, you are truly a piece of work. You're either the smartest woman I know or the luckiest."

"I think it's a combination of both. My decision to call you will be the deal breaker though."

"What do you mean by that?"

"It means, can I count on you to handle the situation without it being traced back to me?"

Mike slowed down his driving and glanced at me. "I know what I'm doing. Having people and things disappear is easier than you think, if you know what you're doing. And you know I know what I'm doing—that's why you called me."

"Can I trust you won't use this against me in the future?"

"I can't promise you that." I shook my head in disgust. "I knew I couldn't trust you."

"Of course you can't, just like I can't trust you. But you calling me to get you out of this dilemma is taking us one step closer to that. Trust is earned and through this incident we are earning each other's trust. I didn't have to help you, and you didn't have to ask for my help, but you did. So now we share something of importance."

"So why did you help me? What do you get out of it?"

"Hopefully, you. It's quite obvious that I've wanted you since the moment I saw you in that club. That hasn't changed. I've been patient, only because I know you're worth the wait."

"I can't get involved with you. It would never work."

"You say that now, but a month ago if someone said I would be helping you get rid of a body, you would've spit in their face. Now here we are driving off together, sharing a secret that could now send both of us to jail. So, never say never."

I put my head down, knowing that he was right. If I was honest with myself, I could see me and Mike in a relationship. The same way he wanted me the first time he saw me in the club, I had a strong attraction to him. But I was in love with Supreme then, and I knew he was the man for me. It didn't stop the lure of Mike. The main road block between us was that he was treacherous. Two treacherous people together were a lethal combination. Look what happened between me and Nico. I didn't want or need that sort of drama again. But then again, never say never.

You Can't Wife a Ho

It had been a week since Mike came through and saved the day. I had only spoken to him once after that, and it was when he called letting me know not to worry because my uncle was in a peaceful place. Which meant B-Boy's cousin was somewhere buried in no man's land. After going through the dead man's wallet, his New York license said his government name was Antwon O'Neal. He was from the boogie down Bronx. I knew his family would be looking for him, including Nico since that was his heroin connect. I wondered if Nico was in on Antwon's scheme to kill me, or if he planned on sharing the news with his long time buddy after dismembering my body. It was irrelevant now. Antwon was dead and gone, while I lived. In the middle of my pondering, I was interrupted by my cell phone ringing. "Hello."

"Hi, Precious, it's me Jamal."

"How are you?"

"Good. I was calling to see if you were still up for that dinner I promised?"

"That's right, how could I forget about that invitation."

"Yeah, because Nina is looking forward to meeting you."

"Nina, your fiancée, of course. When would you like for me to come over?"

"I know it's last minute but how about tonight?"

"Tonight, why not, what time?"

"Is eight okay?"

"No problem."

"You have a pen?"

"Hold on." I grabbed a pen and wrote down his address. I was curious about Jamal's fiancée, but mentally I wasn't really up to meeting her tonight. So much other shit was on mind. Killing Antwon, figuring out Nico's whereabouts, but mostly Mike. I couldn't get him off my mind. He was cold and calculating, but I knew underneath that he had a gentle side. He had so many layers, and each one was so intriguing. I had never met anyone like Mike before. He was the first kingpin I knew who was able to really take the game to a legitimate level and make even more paper. The nigga was huge in the music business. He had mad respect in the industry but still managed to generate that same love from the streets. He had the best of both worlds. He was a hustler for real.

All that said, I still felt I needed to fall back. My heart was still aching over Supreme's death, and I reasoned that that pain would never stop. One day I would have to move on and find a man that could hold it down for me, but I wasn't ready yet. I held on tightly to my pink diamond heart. "Love for life."

When I arrived at Jamal's condo at Trump Place on Riverside Boulevard, I was in awe. "Damn that nigga really came up," I said to myself. His condo was spacious with high ceilings and a banging view of the Hudson River. All that studying and hitting them books had really paid off.

"Jamal, your place is crazy. I'm really proud of you."

"That means a lot to me." I gave Jamal a quizzical look because for the first time it really dawned on me how much my approval meant to him. Realizing that also made me feel guilty about how I kicked him to the curb after I sexually turned him out. But he had moved on. So I guess everything worked out for the best.

"Where's the soon-to-be blushing bride?"

"She's finishing up in the kitchen."

"Oh, she cooks, too. How nice." I hoped my sarcasm wasn't detected.

"Here's my beautiful wife now." I almost wanted to scream. When Nina walked up, I was quite impressed. She was very pretty. With her brown skin, long, coal black hair and exotic features she put me in the mind of Beverly Johnson back in her supermodel days.

"It's nice to meet you. Jamal has told me so much about you," Nina said, shaking my hand.

"I'm sure not everything."

"Yes, he's shared it all," Miss Nina stated with much confidence in her voice. With her pleated pants and white cotton button-down shirt, she seemed all prim and proper, but Nina had some gangsta in her. Trust, I knew a gangstress when I saw one. "So, Precious, would you like something to drink?"

"Actually, this bag in my hand is a bottle of vintage Dom Perignon."

"Thank you, that's so nice."

"Can't come to someone's home empty-handed." The real reason I brought my own liquor was because I don't trust a bitch. She might spit in my shit. We were going to open this bottle right here in my view.

"I'll take that and put it in the refrigerator, so it can get nice and cold."

"No need, it's already chilled. You can just get some glasses and we're good to go." Nina didn't flinch when she turned to go get the champagne glasses. The chick handled herself with coolness.

"I see why you're so smitten. Nina is something else," I

stated, turning to Jamal.

After drinking some champagne we sat down at the table for dinner. I was leery about eating her food, but she laid it out buffet style and I figured we were all digging from the same plate, so if she fucked up my food she fucked up hers, too. I doubted she would torture herself like that.

"How's everything?" she asked.

"Wonderful, baby," Jamal said, reaching over and lovingly rubbing her hand.

"Yeah, these mashed potatoes are incredible. I need to learn how to cook."

"Especially if you plan on keeping a man." Nina smiled then caught the glare coming from Jamal. "I'm so sorry, Precious, how rude of me. It slipped my mind that you recently lost your husband. Please forgive me," Nina pleaded, sounding sincere.

"No apology necessary. So how did you guys meet?" After Nina's comment it had gotten way too intense, and I needed to get the spotlight off me.

"On the set of a music video," Jamal said with a big grin on his face.

"I was playing one of the leads and Jamal stopped by to see how the shoot was going, and we clicked."

Ain't this some shit? I knew that whole librarian persona she was trying to pull off was some bullshit. It was all making sense. That bitch probably performed bedroom tricks on Jamal that he had only seen in porno movies. When we fucked we were young and inexperienced. I was hardly the pro and neither was he. Between Rhonda and Supreme I knew how those chicks on the video sets were putting it down. Most rappers that had any sort of clout wouldn't even let a bitch step foot on the set unless she was coming out those thongs and getting down on her knees.

"How nice, so was that the first video you worked on?"

"No, it was my fourth or fifth. It was my first for Atomic

Records though." Just like I thought, a *ho*-ffessional.

"I'm glad I stopped by that day, or I wouldn't have met my future wife." Nina leaned over and gave Jamal a passionate kiss on the lips. Jamal was in way over his head. He wasn't ready for the type of tricks this bitch had up her sleeves. I hoped she didn't have him too open, but my female intuitions told me she did.

I lingered around and made idle chat until the bottle of Dom P. was finished. I enjoyed talking to Jamal but Nina was getting on my damn nerves with all that mushy shit. She was trying way too hard to come off as some loving, doting girlfriend. It was making me nauseated. Especially since I knew she was nothing more than a paper chaser who had lucked up and found a long-term sponsor in Jamal. Now understand, I wasn't hating on the chick's hustle, because I was the queen of hustle. What bothered me most was her phony ass acting all sweet and innocent when in actuality she was a straight up ho. If she was running this game on any other man, I'd tell her to get that money, but she wasn't. She was doing this to Jamal. He was my first. Nah, I was never in love with the nigga, not even puppy love, but I always admired his intelligence and respected his drive. To see him taken for a ride by some scandalous two-cent video chick was rubbing me the wrong way. But then again, who was I to judge?

"Thank you for having me over, and Nina, dinner was incredible. It's getting late, and I really need to get home."

"Are you okay to drive? You had a few glasses of champagne."

"No, my driver's downstairs waiting. I'm in good hands." Jamal gave me a hug goodnight, and Nina and I gave each other fake hugs and air kisses. That bitch really thought she was about to start living the glamorous life.

The next day, I was in the den reading over the documents my lawyer had drawn up to give to Atomic Records.

We were seeking millions of dollars for them to buy the rights to Supreme's music, but something was telling me to hold up before signing over part of his legacy. I wasn't sure if I wanted to hand over what I considered to be the last piece of Supreme's soul. In the midst of my mulling over my decision, I heard Anna calling for me. "I'm in the den, Anna."

"Mrs. Mills, there is a woman by the name of Nina on the phone for you." *Why in the fuck is Nina calling me?* I thought to myself.

"Thanks, I'll pick up the call in here." I paused and stared at the phone for a moment, wondering what the trick had up her sleeve. "What up, Nina?"

"Hi, Precious. I hope you don't mind me calling, but it was Jamal's suggestion." *Hmm, blame it on your fiancé.* "We have floor seats to the Knicks game, but something came up and Jamal can't make it. He thought I should invite you."

"I think I'll pass."

"I don't want to go by myself, and I would hate to waste these tickets—they're very expensive."

"I'm sure, but you don't have no homegirls you can call?"

"No, I've never had a lot of female friends. That's why Jamal suggested I call you. He speaks so highly of you, Precious. He thinks we would get along great. Please, I really don't want the tickets to go to waste."

I let out a deep sigh, dreading going anywhere with Miss Nina. My gut told me she was bad news, not for me, but for Jamal. I guess it wouldn't kill me to go with her; at least I could get a better idea what her real intentions were regarding him. "Fine, I'll go. What time should I be ready?"

"Thank you so much. You can meet me at my place around six-thirty. We can leave from here."

"Oh, I thought that was Jamal's place, moved in already?"

"Pretty much, I'm basically here all the time."

"Well, I'll see you at six-thirty." I hung up the phone and realized I only had a couple of hours before it would be time to go.

Surprisingly the traffic wasn't that bad, and I arrived at Jamal's place right on time. I figured I would drive so I called Nina and told her to come downstairs. She strutted out the building with a form fitting top and skin tight pants. I guess since Jamal wasn't around she could leave her librarian outfit at home. "Damn, this shit is hot," Nina said admiring my baby blue Bentley.

"Thanks."

"Damn, you really came off marrying Supreme. I know you must be living fly. I didn't get to attend y'all's wedding, but I heard it was like that. Plus I saw the pictures in '*In Style*' magazine."

"Yeah, it's hard to think about all that, when a few months later you're attending your husband's funeral." Nina put her head down with a look of shame for making such a shallow comment.

When we sat down courtside mad heads were in the place. I had never been to a Knicks game but the shit was cool. It was a totally different vibe than watching it on television. With the music, amped crowd and all the celebrities it felt more like a party, only the lights were on. With the players dribbling the ball up and down the court, it was weird having them up close in your face like that.

"You know I used to mess with one of the players on the Knicks." Nina sounded as if she was trying to brag when she made the admission.

"Good for you," I responded nonchalantly.

"He wasn't no star player though, just a benchwarmer. If I could've landed a superstar like Stephon Marbury, I would've hit the jackpot. But somebody beat me to him. He's married. His wife is beautiful, too, her name is Tasha. She be at the games all the time. Could you see yourself marrying a basketball player, Precious?"

"Nah, my men need a little gangsta wit' them. Like Nas say, 'Make sure he's a thug and intelligent too.'"

"I feel you. I love me a thug-ass nigga." I turned all the way around in my seat and gave Nina the craziest look. We both knew that Jamal was as intelligent as they come, but a thug he was not. "I mean I used to like thugs, before I fell in love with Jamal," she said, trying to do damage control. I knew I was right about Nina. She was acting like the hot box that she was now that Jamal was nowhere in sight. The true Nina was showing her face, and all I could do was shake my head. Jamal had his head so far up in Nina's pussy there was no way to warn him about his trifling fiancée. He would just have to find out the hard way. A ho could only hide her stripes but for so long. Hopefully Jamal would figure that out before walking down the aisle with the hussy. If not, it wouldn't be too long before they ended up in divorce court.

After the game Nina and I stopped by the Garden's bar and restaurant where the courtside ticket-holders kicked it. By the time I finished my second drink, I was ready to go home. As I drove Nina home she made it clear that she didn't want the night to end. "One of the players for the Knicks is having an after party at Taj. We should go."

"I'm tired, plus I'm sure Jamal is ready for you to come home."

"He had to go out of town—that was the something that came up. So I don't have to get home no time soon."

"I hear you, but I'm beat. I have to get up early in the morning so I really need to get home."

"That's too bad, but we can always hang out another time. I think we could be good friends, Precious."

"Sweetheart, I don't have friends."

"That's too bad."

"Bad for who?"

"For you. Everyone needs somebody." By this time I was pulling up to the Trump Place. "I really had a nice time with you. I hope we can go out again together."

"Maybe."

"I'll give you a call. Bye, Precious."

"Bye." I watched Nina walk up the stairs, and I decided she wasn't that bad. She was somewhat funny, and I had to admit that I enjoyed myself. I couldn't really be mad at the chick for trying to find a long-term sponsor in Jamal. If I didn't know him, I would probably be cheering her on. Shit, living in New York is a hard knock life; you got to fit in where you can get in. Maybe a ho don't make a good wife, but they make for an excellent partying partner.

You Will be Mine

After keeping my distance from Mike for the next couple of months, one day he decided to pay me a surprise visit. "Precious, you have a visitor," Nathan announced with an attitude.

"Who is it?"

"That cat, Mike."

"What the hell is he doing here?" I knew I shouldn't have let him know where I lived.

"I don't know. I'll be more than happy to send him away."

"That's okay. The guards checked him up front?"

"Yeah, he clean." I followed Nathan downstairs, upset that Mike would show up to my home unannounced. I was even more upset with myself for having butterflies in my stomach.

"What are you doing here?" I asked Mike as he stood in the foyer.

"Is that anyway to greet a friend?"

"When I see a friend I'll ask him."

"Cute, let's talk," Mike said, putting his arm around my waist and escorting me toward the den. Nathan immediately stepped forward and pushed his arm away.

"Don't nobody touch Precious," Nathan snapped at Mike.

"Nathan, it's okay."

"I apologize. I didn't mean to offend you. But in the future, just so you know, nobody touches me either," said Mike with the most endearing smile on his face while his eyes spoke a language of deadliness.

"Mike, you shouldn't have come here without calling first," I said, closing the door to the den.

"If you answered my calls, I would've."

"I've been busy."

"Busy doing what?"

"Just things."

"Stop dancing around my question and answer it," Mike demanded.

"I know this may come as a surprise to you, but you don't tell me what to do. Other people may have to answer to you, but I don't. Don't think because I turned to you for help that now I have to bow down like you own me. That'll never happen. I've been busy, and that's the only explanation you need."

"You know what I told you about the word 'never.' But besides that, I think you're avoiding me." Mike walked over to me.

"Why would I need to avoid you?" I turned my back to him, pretending to look for something.

"Because of how I make you feel," Mike whispered in my ear. I was taking in the alluring smell of his cologne as he stood next to me. I wanted to push him away and tell him that I never wanted to see him again, but my body wouldn't let me. It had only been a few months since Supreme's death, but I was drawn to Mike, and I also missed the comfort of having affection from a man.

"I think you should go," I managed to say.

"Stop trying to fight it. Give in to your feelings." Mike's

soft lips sprinkled kisses up my neck until he came to my mouth. His hands were slowly gliding up my thighs and in that moment I gave into the temptation. We began to passionately kiss, and he pushed me toward the mahogany desk. Mike pushed the papers out the way and sat me down and gently separated my legs. As our kisses became more intense the tingle that was once going through my entire body had moved to my pussy. Mike slid my panties to the side and massaged my warm clit with his finger. Then he took it a step further, sliding his thick, long fingers inside of me. His finger fucking had my hips rocking to the rhythm of his strokes.

"Do you want to feel the real thing?"

"Yes," I said breathlessly. I couldn't wait to wrap my legs around Mike's muscular body and feel all of him inside of me. As he unzipped his pants all of a sudden he just stopped. "What's wrong?" I asked in confusion.

"We can't do this."

"If you're worried about someone coming in, the door is locked. No one can disturb us." I started kissing Mike again because my pussy was now on fire.

"It's not that."

"Then what?"

"I don't want to have sex with you like this."

"I don't understand."

"I've been dying to feel inside of you."

"Well, here's your chance." I opened my legs wider and pulled him closer.

"Not like this. When I have you it won't be in some moment of lust that you'll regret right after we finish. No, you'll be mine, and you'll enjoy every moment, before, during and after. I won't settle for anything less." Mike zipped his pants back up, and I grabbed his hand.

"Don't do this. You got me all fuckin' open and now you wanna shut me off. This is bullshit. You can't just leave me out here like this."

"Precious, you want some dick, that's all."

"No, it's not like that. I don't just want dick. I want it from you." Mike bit down on his bottom lip as if imagining us fucking. With the lust in his eyes I thought he had changed his mind and was about to put it on me. But instead he rubbed his fingers through my hair and held it tightly. "Mike, that hurts."

"I know, but I want your full attention when I tell you this." He was looking at me so seriously, and I wondered how I let myself get caught up in Mike's games. "Get your mind right, because you will be mine. Sooner rather than later, and when you step into my world, Precious, the stakes are much higher." Mike gave me one last kiss and walked out leaving me completely frustrated. I had dealt with several thugs in my life, but Mike was on a whole other level. He was the first man who somewhat intimidated me. It wasn't a feeling I was comfortable with, but I also knew it was one I would have to explore.

That night as I undressed to take a shower, I stood in front of the mirror admiring my body. I was finally back to my perfect size six and the surgery the plastic surgeon performed on my scar was off the chain. It healed beautifully and the slight mark was barely noticeable. I was very impressed and knew that Mike would be, too, once he decided to stop playing mind games and we finally got naked. He was trying to make the situation so complicated. After fighting it for so long, the moment I wanted to give in to lust he makes me wait. It wasn't surprising though, Mike had to be in control of everything. He made it clear that having my body wasn't enough. He wanted my mind, and more than likely, my soul.

Ring...ring...
"Hello."

"Precious, I know it's early but I need to speak to you."

The voice on the other end was Jamal, and I was pissed he was waking me up so early in the morning.

"Jamal, this better be good."

"I was hoping we could meet for breakfast. We need to talk."

"About what? What is so important that it couldn't wait until at least ten?"

"It's about Nina."

"I know you're not interrupting my sleep over your fiancée?"

"Please, can I come over?"

"Fine."

"I'll be there in an hour." Before I could get out another word the line was dead. I dragged myself out of bed still wondering why Jamal felt it was so urgent to speak to me regarding Nina. After getting dressed I went downstairs where I was greeted with a room full of flowers.

"Mrs. Mills, all these came for you first thing this morning. A truck pulled up full of flowers," Anna explained.

"Was there a card?"

"Yes, I'll get it for you." As Anna went to get the card I stood admiring the beautiful flower arrangements. Everything from red rose compositions to multicolored mini calla lilies filled up the foyer. I had never seen such an array of flowers before. Anna handed me the card, which read:

Dinner tonight, be ready at eight.
- Mike

That was it—no romantic poems or declaring his undying love. Mike was as cool as they came. "Somebody's very fond of you, Mrs. Mills." Anna smiled, obviously digging for dirt.

"I suppose," I said, walking to each bouquet taking in the aroma of the fresh flowers. "A friend of mine should be here any minute, could you please make us breakfast? We'll be eating in the den."

"Of course." Before Anna could head to the kitchen, Jamal was coming around the corner.

"Damn, did you fly over here?"

"Wow, is someone having a wedding today?" Jamal was too taken aback by the flowers to answer my question. "Look at this place. I've never seen so many flowers in someone's home before. This is crazy."

"Tell me about it." He, like Anna, was way more excited than I was.

"They're all for you?"

"Yep."

"I assume it's from a man, and he obviously has it bad for you."

"We'll see. Enough about me. I want to know why you woke me up early this morning. Let's go in the den, Anna is going to bring us breakfast."

"I'm not hungry, but thanks for seeing me. You're one of the few people I feel I can confide in."

"What's wrong?" From Jamal's demeanor, it was obvious something was weighing heavily on his mind.

"It's Nina. Her behavior just doesn't seem quite right to me."

"What do you mean not quite right, like mentally?"

"No, no, no," Jamal said as he shook his head. "I think she might be seeing someone else." Nina seeing someone else wouldn't be a major surprise to me, but I figured she would be more discreet with it, never taking the chance that Jamal would find out. I mean, he was her ticket out of the trailers on video sets to a penthouse in the sky.

"Who?"

"That, I don't know."

"So you don't have any proof, just a hunch?"

"More than a hunch, sometimes she goes missing during the day. I'll call her at home or on her cell, and she doesn't pick up. When she finally returns my call, her excuses are either she was in an area with no reception or she left her phone somewhere and just got it back. Just silly excuses that would work once in a while but not all the time."

"Have you confronted her about your suspicions?"

"Yeah, and of course she denies it. When I go a little deeper with the interrogation she always starts to pleasure me in the way that only she can." As Jamal continued to talk with his head down, I rolled my eyes. Nina was a girl after my own heart. She definitely had her game intact. When in trouble with your man, sex him right to make him forget all suspicions. Unfortunately for her, Jamal's forgetting only lasted momentarily.

"Hire a private investigator to follow her."

"I did."

"And?"

"She takes the train, and he always loses her. Her cell phone records don't show any suspicious number."

"The train? Nina strikes me as the type of person who would've given that up once she moved in with you."

"That's the thing. When she goes shopping or is running errands, she either takes a cab or uses my car service. But at least three times a week she takes the train. I find that odd. It's as if she's purposely trying to get lost just in case someone is following her."

"That's interesting. So what are you going to do?"

"Precious, I was hoping you could help me." Jamal lifted his head and turned to face me, staring at me with begging eyes. At that moment I saw the old Jamal from the Brooklyn projects looking at me. He seemed almost fragile.

"What can I do?"

"Befriend Nina. She really enjoyed herself when you all went to the Knicks game. Nina likes you, Precious, she told me. But she said you told her you don't have any friends— I'm hoping that's not true. I'm hoping that you think of me as a friend, and will help me out."

"I don't know, Jamal. I have so much going on in my own life and wasting time with Nina doesn't fit into my schedule."

"Make it fit. It wouldn't be a waste of time. I might be totally wrong about Nina, or I might not. But if I am, marrying her would be the worst thing I could ever do. I need to know. Our wedding is less than two months away."

"Okay. I'll do it."

"Thank you so much, Precious. I'll never forget this."

"Don't get so excited. She might not confide anything to me. Remember she knows that we're cool." Jamal gave me a million dollar smile.

"If anybody can get to the bottom of something, it's you. I'm confident you'll find out what is going on, if anything. So how about calling Nina now and maybe having a girls' night out?"

"I can't tonight, I already have plans." Disappointment immediately spread across Jamal's face. "I will call her and set something up for tomorrow." The disappointment instantly changed to delight. Jamal walked over and hugged me tightly.

"It's too bad we never had a chance to see if a relationship could've worked between us, because you're perfect."

"Jamal, I'm not perfect, nobody is. Remember that."

"I know, but you're as close to perfect as one can get." We both smiled, and I walked Jamal out. It was amazing how everybody in your life could view you differently. But then again I seemed to show a different side of myself to each person. With Jamal, I always showed him the respectable lady in me. That's why he constantly put me on a pedestal. But then again maybe that's the side he brought out, because he was such a gentleman. Jamal would be shocked to know that with everyone else in my life I was a straight up bitch, and that was on my good days.

After eating my breakfast, I placed the call to Nina.

"Hi, it's me, Precious."

"Precious, it's so nice to hear from you. I left you a few messages, but you never called me back."

"I'm sorry. I had so much going on, and I actually had to go out of town for a few weeks." That was a lie, but it sounded good. "But now I'm back and was hoping maybe we could get together tomorrow?"

"Girl, yes, there's this new restaurant I heard about. It's supposed to be hot. We should go."

"Sounds good, I'll pick you up tomorrow night around seven-thirty."

"Perfect. I knew we would be friends, Precious. We're two of a kind." On that note I ended the call. Nina truly believed it was all gravy with us. Under different circumstances we might have been cool, but at the same time, her personality was always so happy-go-lucky. Shit like that made me suspicious. I mean damn, most everybody got problems, and those who don't are the ones starting them.

As it got later in the day I started preparing for my date with Mike. I was looking forward to spending some quality time with him. I had never sat down and just kicked it with Mike on some relaxing shit.

Standing in front of the mirror fixing my hair, instead of my own reflection staring back at me it was Supreme's. It was probably because of the guilt I felt. "Baby, I know Mike ain't never been one of your favorite dudes, but I kinda dig him. I'm so lonely, Supreme, and it's hard for me. I wake up every day thinking of you, and go to sleep every night wishing you were beside me. Mike can never take your place in my heart, but I think we're somewhat compatible. The streets run through his blood just like they do mine. Most people just don't understand that about me, but Mike does. I hope you understand, and you don't hold it against me, because with us, it's love for life." I spoke those words to

Supreme as if he were standing before me in the flesh. His presence was always felt, and somewhere in my mind I did believe he could hear me. Maybe it was because of the necklace he gave me that I never took off. Whatever it was, the connection was strong.

After going back and forth over how to rock my hair—up then down then up again—I let my golden brown waves hang loosely down my shoulders. I put on my fitted cream pantsuit and pulled out the shearling to match. It was exactly eight, and I knew Mike would be right on time. I went downstairs to have a quick drink before he arrived. Nathan was standing in the foyer as if he was waiting for me. "Good evening, Nathan," I said with a pleasant smile.

"You need me to escort you somewhere tonight?" he asked in a protective tone.

"No, I'm fine."

"So where are you going?"

"Out," I replied, trying to remain cool. I never liked for anyone to question me. But I knew Nathan was asking out of concern, so I didn't want to bite his head off.

"With who?" He asked one question too many, and now he was working my nerves.

"That's really none of your business, but if you must know, Mike."

"Pretty Boy Mike? Why do you deal with that arrogant nigga? You know Supreme wouldn't approve of him."

"Nathan, for one, Supreme is no longer with us. Two, I'm grown. I don't have to explain to you or anybody else who I choose to deal with. As far as approval goes, mine is the only one that counts. Now, excuse me, my date is here," I said, hearing the doorbell ring.

Even after the tongue lashing I just gave Nathan, he lingered behind me as I answered the door. He glared at Mike with hatred in his eyes. I tried to ignore his stares, but it was hard since Nathan wasn't exactly unnoticeable.

"Precious, you look beautiful," Mike said, ignoring the wannabe cock blocker.

"Thanks, let's get out of here." I turned to Nathan, "Have a good night, and don't wait up."

When we pulled up to 23rd Street I wondered where Mike was taking me for dinner. The block was lined with elegant buildings more suited for private residences than restaurants. "Where are we going?" I finally asked.

"Bette. It's Amy Sacco's restaurant. She owns Bungalow 8, this exclusive nightclub I go to sometimes."

"Oh, I've never heard of either of those places."

"Well, I'm the first to show you something different."

"What type of food do they serve?"

"European grill. It's delicious, trust me."

When we entered the spot, I was impressed by the elegant but yet sleek style. It had smoked glass with amber and charcoal colors. The Mobius-inspired tubular light fixture gave it an ultra modern, high-tech 70s look. I let Mike do the ordering since I didn't know what was good on the menu. He got some herb-grilled black sea bass and some braised short ribs, which sounded delicious to me. We started things off with a bottle of bubbly, just the way I like.

"So I guess you want to wine and dine me before you sleep with me, huh?"

"It's not so much that. I want us to really get to know each other. I think you're special, Precious, and you're someone I want in my life on a long-term basis."

"I don't know if that's possible."

"Why not?"

"Because you knew and know two of the men who have had the biggest impact on my life. It might be too complicated."

"Listen, Supreme is no longer with us, may he rest in peace, and Nico isn't a part of my life. I want to have the biggest impact on your life, in a positive way. I can see us sharing an incredible life together. I can show you things that you've never been exposed to. There is so much out there, Precious, and I want you to experience it as my wife."

"What?" I almost choked on the champagne going down my throat.

"You heard me." Mike paused as he leaned back in his chair. With his caramel complexion glowing under the light, he ran his fingers over his perfect full lips. "It's my hope that one day soon you'll become my wife."

"I just lost my husband less than a year ago. I have no plans to remarry anytime soon, if ever."

"So you have no problem having sex with me on a desk, but you don't want to consider marrying me one day?"

"Sex is totally different than being somebody's wife. We don't even really know each other."

"They say you know if you want to marry somebody within the first moments of meeting them. I never believed that to be true until I met you. Unfortunately, you're afraid of letting your guard down with me. I can't blame you, under the circumstances. It'll take time. But like any great stock, you have to invest. I'm willing to invest in you, because I believe the benefits are worthwhile."

"I'll admit that I'm extremely attracted to you. Not just physically but mentally. You seem to understand me, and at the same time not judge me. There was something about you from the moment I met you, and I think it's because I see so much of myself in you, which is a little frightening. I don't have the most endearing qualities."

"To me, Precious, you're perfect. The qualities you say are lacking in endearment are what I find most appealing. That is the reason you will be mine. I'll put money on it."

Mike and I ate our dinner as he talked to me about everything from the music business to great investments. He was truly well schooled. He told me the street life was the best form of education he ever received to prepare him for the cutthroat corporate world.

By the time we finished, we had gone through two bottles of champagne and I was tipsy. As we waited for the valet to pull the car around, I caught the side profile of a woman about to go into an apartment a few buildings down. "Is that Nina?" I asked out loud.

"Who is Nina?" Mike questioned as he walked in my direction and put his hand around my waist. I shook my head because I was so drunk I could barely stand up straight.

"Just someone I know," I replied, glancing back over to where I saw her. But when I turned around she was gone.

"Where? I don't see anybody," Mike said, peering in the direction I had my head turned.

"Me neither, I think my eyes were just playing tricks on me. That's what happens when you have too much to drink."

Mike and I got in the car, and he took me home. When he reached my house I didn't want him to leave. "Would you like to come in?"

"No, you need to get some rest. I'll call you tomorrow."

"Okay." Mike walked me to the door, and I was disappointed that our night was ending. I really enjoyed his company and looked forward to spending more time with him. "Thanks, Mike," I said before giving him a kiss goodnight. When I walked inside, Nathan was sitting in the corner pretending to be flipping through a magazine.

"Enjoy your evening?" Nathan asked with his head still buried in the magazine.

"Didn't I tell you not to wait up for me? Don't answer that, just don't do it again." I went upstairs and closed my bedroom door. Even in my drunken stupor I knew that one day soon I would need to have a serious talk with Nathan. I had to set some rules regarding him interfering with my personal life, especially since I had the feeling Mike would soon become a big part of it.

In Da Club

I woke up the next morning with a newfound anticipation. It was due to the wonderful evening I had shared with Mike the night before and the many possibilities it raised. The depressing, not wanting to get out of bed feeling that I had to fight for months after Supreme died was gone. I was looking forward to my next date with Mike and what the future might hold for us.

Ring…ring…

The sound of my cell phone interrupted my daydreaming.

"Hello."

"Precious, it's me, Nina. I wanted to make sure we were still on tonight?" I fell back in bed, closing my eyes. It slipped my mind that I was supposed to hang with Nina tonight. But I did promise Jamal, and I couldn't let him down.

"Of course, we're still on."

"Great, I already made reservations for us at this new hot spot. We're going to have so much fun. I'll see you tonight." Before I had a chance to roll my eyes about Nina's extra bubbly ass, my cell phone rang again.

"Hello."

"Good morning." Without even thinking I started grinning at the sound of Mike's voice.

"Good morning to you." I couldn't help but wonder if the tone of my voice gave away the smile on my face.

"It will be if you say you'll see me again tonight."

"Mike, I can't. I already have plans with a girlfriend of mine."

"You have a female friend? I had no idea," he said, sounding surprised.

"She's more of an associate, but nevertheless we're going out tonight."

"You can't reschedule with her? I have something for you."

"As tempting as that sounds, unfortunately these plans are unbreakable. Maybe tomorrow or another day this week?"

"We'll work something out. I'll give you a call later on. Enjoy your evening." I was furious that I had to hang out with Nina all night when I could be with Mike. But Jamal needed me, and if anyone deserved my help it was him.

With so much going on, I hadn't been focusing on finding Nico. It seemed all my leads had dried up. The police weren't making any headway and even the private investigators that Supreme had hired before his death were hitting dead ends. It was becoming frustrating. I did want to see where things could go between me and Mike, but I wouldn't truly be able to go on with my life until I got retribution for what Nico did to Supreme. But I knew patience was what this situation required. If you keep putting questions out there, sooner or later, the answers find their way to you. Eventually Nico and I would have our showdown, and my face would be the last he'd see when I gave him the kiss of death.

"This place is cute, Nina," I commented when we walked right in to the slick two-level club/lounge in the Meatpacking district.

"Isn't it? The who's who always come to this spot. Getting a table is damn near impossible, but with Jamal's connections it was smooth sailing. Now that he is the president of Atomic Records, everywhere I go I get red carpet treatment." *Red carpet,* I thought to myself, *this chick is straight tripping. Talk about Hollywood, Nina acting like she's Halle Berry or some shit like that. Unfuckingbelievable.*

"Yeah, it seems pretty exclusive," I said, noticing Janet Jackson and Jermaine Dupri at a corner table. "What's the name of this spot again?"

"AER. Do you want to stay up here or go downstairs?" Nina inquired.

"It's up to you."

"I'll show you around then we'll come back upstairs, because this is where our table is." I followed Nina downstairs and the spot felt like an intimate private VIP room. The floor was transparent with a pulsing video projection underneath. Lining the room were plush suede couches with Lucite armrests. Nina then showed me two smaller rooms, one with nothing but a few antique throne chairs and a movie playing on the wall. The spot was definitely official.

After Nina gave me the tour we went back upstairs and Young Jeezy's new single was blasting from the speakers. The crowd was dancing on the thickly upholstered ottomans and when they would come up for air, they'd grab a drink from the metallic cocktail tables. Some other patrons were getting their party on by dancing on the banquettes and the carpeted platform that wrapped around the room. The 'it' crowd was predominately white with a sprinkle of black people, but the music was all hip hop so I was cool.

The moment we sat down, the waiter approached with two magnums. "Nina, did you order some champagne before we got here?"

"Nah," she said shaking her head.

"Sir, we didn't order no champagne, at least not yet."

"These are complimentary," he replied.

"From who?"

"Who cares?" Nina said with her face lighting up. "It's free, and top of the line bubbly." Nina broke out into a little cele-bratory dance, grinding in her chair. "Can you pour me a glass?" The waiter obliged and poured both of us a glass. In the middle of her sipping, Nina nudged my arm. I turned in the direction she was nodding her head to see what looked like some NBA players walking through the entrance.

"I told you, Nina, I only fuck wit' thug niggas."

"First of all, there are a lot of athletes that's straight gangsta with theirs."

"Name me one?" I gave Nina the screw face waiting for her answer.

"Allen Iverson." Nina paused and stared at me. "Him, and all his people carry heat." That I could believe. I didn't know who too many basketball players were, but I could see Allen Iverson being 'bout it, 'bout it.

"Whatever, he ain't in that crowd, besides he's married with enough kids to start his own NBA team."

"Girl, you so crazy. I'm engaged anyway. I was just play-ing with you, but it doesn't hurt to just flirt a little bit. We're just having fun." I continued to drink my champagne as Nina made eye contact with one of the players. To her delight they were seated at a booth across from us. Before long the dudes were offering us drinks and shit, even though we had two big-ass bottles sitting on our table. But Nina didn't care—she accepted them anyway. Then they started motioning their hands for us to come join them, and I pre-tended that I didn't see that shit.

"Precious, they want us to join them. Let's go over there." Nina was all giddy. I really wanted to scream at Nina and tell her I didn't think Jamal would approve of her ho-ass antics. But I was trying to befriend her so she'd feel comfortable to do and say anything she pleased around me.

"Hell no, I'm not about to sit at a table with a bunch of niggas and ain't none of them my man."

"Stop being so uptight. It doesn't hurt to play a little bit as long as you know where to draw the line. I'm committed to Jamal, and I wouldn't do anything to jeopardize that."

"I hear you, Nina, but still. If they want to talk to us they can come over here." I didn't know if the niggas read my lips or were just mind readers, but before I even completed my sentence three of the guys strolled over to our table.

"How you ladies doing?" the ringleader said as he extended his arm. Nina shook his hand, and I just nodded my head and smiled. Shoot, I didn't know what he had been touching on before he came over to see us. "Can we have a seat?"

"Sure," Nina responded before I had an opportunity to shut them down. But it was a good thing they came over. Now I could see how far Nina planned on taking her so-called flirtation. "I'm Nina, and this is Precious."

"How you doing fellas?" I asked casually.

"Better after meeting you ladies. I'm Keith and these my boys Jalen and Mark."

"What's up?" the once mute fellas said. I finally took a good look at the three men, and they all had the same style—jeans, a button-up shirt, fresh sneakers and enough bling between them to open up their own jewelry store. They were a variation of browns with low cut hair. Each was above average in the looks department but nothing to make you wanna write home to your mama about.

"So, what do you ladies do?" Keith asked.

"I'm a model. I do music videos and stuff like that." Then Keith looked at me waiting for my answer.

"I don't *do* anything."

"What, you somebody baby mama or something, sitting back collecting checks?"

"Yes, I am collecting checks as a matter of fact, but I ain't anybody's baby mama. How many do you have, while we're on the subject?"

"What you mean by that?"

"What I mean is, how many baby mamas do you have, Keith? Is that question clear enough for you?" The nerve of that nigga stepping to me asking me a question like that, now he wanna act like he don't understand when I throw the shit back at him. Even if I was sitting back collecting checks as somebody's baby mama it wouldn't be none of his business.

"Yeah, it's clear. I actually got three."

"Three kids or three baby mamas?"

"Three baby mamas." Jalen and Mark chuckled a little bit.

"Seems you've been a busy bee. Are they sitting back and collecting checks from you?" I asked sarcastically.

"I'm an NBA player. I make plenty of dough; all my kids are straight." By now, everyone had their eyes glued on us.

"Good for them. Make sure you keep making that money, 'cause you have a few mouths to feed."

"Anyway, back to you." Keith got the hint and started his conversation back up with Nina. See, that was the reason I didn't fuck with athletes. Most of them are some real soft niggas. They were pampered all through high school and then college. They expect everybody to kiss they ass. Then when they go pro and make all these millions the ego becomes out of control. Because they was too busy practicing their hoop game they never truly had to get their hustle on in the streets. I had no time for dudes like that. A bitch like me would have to cut one of them when they crossed my path on some simple-ass shit. Then my face would be spread across every paper in America. Nah, I was better off with my thug niggas.

"So you got a man or what?" one of Keith's friends asked me. I couldn't remember if he was Jalen or Mark, but I knew he might be the one with a little gangsta in him if he was still thirsty for me after I checked his friend.

"No, I'm single."

"We're playing the Knicks tomorrow, and then we fly out. Can I get your number and maybe you can come visit me, since you said you don't really do nothing but collect checks?" We both started laughing.

"Yeah, I did say that, didn't I?"

"No doubt, but that's cool. I don't know if you're into basketball, but I can leave some tickets for you if you wanna see the game. It'll be a blowout, 'cause that's how we do."

"Is that right?"

"That's a promise. Let me take down your number, and I'll call you to set everything up."

"Okay, but I'll need two tickets. I'm bringing Nina."

"No problem, I got you."

"What's your name again?"

"Jalen."

"I like that. You look young, how long you been in the league?"

"This is my fourth year. I got drafted straight out of high school."

"You must be really good."

"Last season I was the league MVP." I decided I might have to make an exception to my athlete rule, because Jalen seemed cool. He was laid back and not so boisterous with his shit. I was feeling his easy-going attitude.

I was beginning to relax and get comfortable kicking it with Jalen, but I still kept my eye on Nina to see just how up-close and personal she was getting with Keith. I caught the occasional fake, sexy laugh she was giving him but nothing else. Then in the middle of Jalen telling me one of his locker room stories I felt the coldest hands pressing down on my shoulders.

"What the fuck," I said, turning my head to see who was testing they life by sneaking up behind me and touching on me. Jalen was just as surprised as me, and immediately stood up as if ready to go to blows for me. He was definitely my type of man.

"Did you enjoy the champagne I got for you?" I instantly recognized the voice.

"Mike, how did you know I was going to be here?"

"Oh, so you know this guy?" Jalen said as he sat back down in his seat.

"Yes, she knows me very well."

"I was speaking to Precious, I don't need your input," Jalen spit.

"Young blood, I think you need to check who you speaking to. I'm not David Stern, and I don't give a fuck about you being the MVP. If you want to keep dribbling that ball correctly stay out of grown people's conversations." It was obvious Mike knew who Jalen was, but poor Jalen had no idea who he was dealing with. I'm not saying that in a one-on-one battle Jalen couldn't hold his own; it was the aftermath I would be worried about. Mike's vicious ass might put a street hit out on Jalen just because.

"Nigga, ain't nobody tripping off of you. You can get it just like the next man. I know how to beat down grown-ass men, too," Jalen said as he stood back up. Then the other three players that were still sitting in their booth got up and came to our table.

"Listen, this is some bullshit. Mike, let's go."

"You leaving with this nigga?" Now Jalen looked like he wanted to whip my ass.

"Yes." *Call me*, I silently mouthed. The last thing I wanted was a brawl. One thing I was sure of, Mike wasn't in here alone. Somewhere close by I'm sure he had some niggas that were strapping, lingering about.

"Come on Nina, let's go."

"Do we have to?"

"Ah...yes, unless you wanna stay here. I'm out."

"Baby, you stay right here, I'll take you home." Keith stood up and put his hand around Nina's arm.

"No, I can't. If Precious is leaving then so am I."

"Fuck her. You ain't gotta leave 'cause her punk-ass man dragging her home. You can chill with me." I just shook my head because I knew it was about to be on.

"My man, what the fuck did you just say?" Mike asked calmly.

"You heard me, and I ain't yo' man, nigga. Nina staying here with me." Keith stood up, all 6'7" of him. He was about five inches taller than Mike, but that didn't mean shit.

"Understand one thing. The only interest I have at this table is Precious. Everybody else is irrelevant to me. But if you keep riffin' wit' yo' mouth like something is sweet over here you gon' have a problem."

"Nigga, bring it on. Do you know who the fuck I am?" It happened so fast. One minute Keith was running off at the mouth, the next he was hitting the floor. All it took was one right hand punch and Mike's fist had Keith laid out. The other players looked like they were ready to jump Mike until three niggas in all black stepped to the table with guns drawn.

"Let's go, now!" I screamed. I grabbed Nina's arm and Mike followed me out the club. When we got to the car I was mad as hell.

"Omigoodness, that was crazy in there," Nina said as if she was star struck off of Mike.

"You always startin' some shit. When I first met yo' ass you was in the middle of that brawl with Supreme's body-guards. That's why Nathan don't like yo' ass now!" I yelled back at Mike as I walked to my car.

"Fuck Nathan. Besides, that nigga in there was out of line. He lucky didn't nobody put a bullet in his head." Mike ran up behind me and grabbed my arm.

"That's what I'm talkin' 'bout right there. There is a time and place for everything. You can't be on no cowboys and

Indians shit up in the club. How did you know I was going to be there anyway?"

"I know everything."

"Whatever. I'm taking Nina home. I'll speak to you later." I released myself from his grip and stormed off.

"Precious, wait."

"What?"

"Don't be mad at me."

"It's a little too late for that."

"I'll admit, I was jealous when I saw you talking to that Jalen nigga. Before tonight, I actually dug his moves on the court, but seriously, I shouldn't have lost my cool in there. Forgive me?" Mike had opened his arms as if I would run and give him a hug.

"Honestly, I'm glad you knocked that nigga Keith on his ass. He was a real pompous motherfucker that needed to be put in his place. But popping up on me like that and flipping out on the dude I was talking to was out of line. I'm not even your girl. You don't have rights to me like that."

"So why did you leave with me?"

"Because I was trying to keep the peace. But if you want to get technical you followed me out."

"Oh, so it wasn't because you feeling me?"

"You already know that I dig you, but that's beside the point. Shit take time, and running up on me like I'm rockin' your ring or some shit ain't the move."

"I apologize. I guess since I already know you're going to be my wife I conduct myself that way." I couldn't help but laugh at Mike's comment. The arrogance that got on my nerves was the same thing that attracted me to him. He was so damn confident, and that shit was sexy as hell.

"Call me tomorrow so you can let me know the next time we're going out," he added.

"Hum...so you think we still going out?" I smirked. Mike just gave me his signature devilish smile and walked away as if he knew I would be calling.

"Girl, who is that nigga? He is sexy as hell," Nina blurted once we got in the car.

"Just a friend."

"He gotta be more than a friend coming for you like that."

"Maybe a little bit more." But after Mike showed his ass in the club, I felt I needed to put the brakes on him for a second.

"He is straight gutter with his. He reminds me of this other dude."

"Who?" I was curious to know. Mike was a rare breed. The only nigga that came close to him was Nico.

"Oh, just some guy I used to know a long time ago," Nina said, brushing over my question. "Precious, you got a winner in him." I ignored Nina's comment and jumped to something else.

"Sorry if I fucked things up for you and Keith."

"Girl, please. He had that shit coming. The whole time he was talking to me he kept going on and on about himself. He was about to put me to sleep. Plus that shit wasn't serious, just a little fun to pass the time. I have a fiancé to go home to."

"I feel you."

"I had a ball with you, Precious, even with all the drama. I can't wait to tell Jamal the story—he gonna bug out," Nina said as I pulled up in front of her building.

"Damn sure is."

"Call me when you feel like hanging out again." Nina waved as she closed the car door.

"Will do." I watched Nina walk inside and couldn't help but laugh. Although in principle this was a favor for Jamal, Nina always tripped me out, and I enjoyed her company. I really didn't have any concrete information to tell Jamal. Nina was definitely a flirt, but maybe she didn't take it any further than that. It was hard to tell and I only wanted to speak on the facts. I would no doubt be hanging out with her in the near future, because I was determined to deliver the good or bad news to Jamal before the wedding date.

What's the 411

As I drove to Madison Square Garden to pick up the tickets Jalen left for me, I couldn't help but think about Supreme when the melodic sounds of Usher's "*U Got It Bad*" played on the radio. I thought about the time he broke up with me because I went missing for a day and couldn't explain my whereabouts. He was furious thinking I was out creeping with some other nigga but in actuality I was out murdering my best friend, Inga, and Nico's hoochie, Porscha. "But how do you tell your man some shit like that?" I asked out loud, laughing as I thought about the answer to my own question.

It had been over six months since Supreme was ripped out of my life, but it hadn't gotten any easier to deal with. Yes, I was going out again and giving other niggas a little life, but it didn't numb the pain in my heart from losing Supreme. When my mother got killed I just knew nothing would ever make me hurt that bad again, until I watched Supreme die right in front of my eyes.

I would never get over Supreme, but it was time to kick it with a dude that could hold me down. I wasn't sure, but my instinct was telling me that Mike could be the one. He understood what type of chick I was and had no desire to change me, but as much as I thought Mike might be the one for me, another part of me was very reluctant. Every time I was around Mike I felt as if he was hiding a dark secret. I knew a man like Mike had his skeletons, but it seemed deeper than that. But maybe it was just my paranoia. I started pondering what life with Mike would be like when I heard my cell ringing.

"Hello," I answered, turning down the car radio.

"I have some information about Nico that I think will interest you." I didn't recognize the female voice on the other end of the phone, but she no doubt had my attention.

"Who is this and how did you get my number?"

"Who I am don't matter, but knowing where Nico is does."

"What, you saying you know where Nico is?"

"Something like that."

"That sounds a little shaky to me. Either you know where Nico is or you're wasting my time and my phone minutes. I'm thinking you one of those silly chicks playing on the phone, but you running game wit' the wrong bitch."

"Before Nico shot you, you told him you didn't want to die, but he said you were already dead and he just came to take it in blood." I took the phone from my ear and glared at it for a long minute. I could hear the girl repeating the word "hello" wondering what the hell happened to me. She fucked me up with that one because I remember those words Nico spoke to me as if he had said them yesterday, and it still sent chills down my spine.

"Yo, you made your point. Where that nigga at?"

"You know it's gonna cost you," she boasted, matter-of-factly.

"Of course, how much you want?" I wasn't sure if the chick had heard about the million dollar ransom floating around on the streets, and I wasn't going to volunteer the information. But I had no problem paying it if it guaranteed I could watch Nico take his last breath.

"How much you offering?" she asked, proving that, yeah, she was holding onto some valuable information, but was definitely a rookie when it came to negotiating for that paper.

"I'll let you know when we meet to discuss Nico's whereabouts."

"Who said I wanted to meet you in person?" Her voice had an underlying nervousness in it.

"Well what, you want me to FedEx your money?"

"Nah, I just need to think this through a little more. I'll be in touch."

"Wait!" I yelled, but she'd already hung up. She called from a blocked number so I couldn't even dial her back. My insides were burning up. My gut told me she knew exactly where Nico was, if not the precise location, then enough to lead me in the right direction. I kept replaying our conversation trying to figure out what I said that scared her off. At first she sounded so confident, but when she realized it was about to go down she froze up. I guess it kicked in that she was rumbling with big dogs so she punked out. I kept my fingers crossed that the idea of having some real cheddar in her hands would motivate the girl to call back.

After picking up the tickets for that night's game and running some other errands, it was time for me to scoop up Nina. Her wedding to Jamal was fast approaching, and I was somewhat relieved that I didn't have any scandalous news to break to him. I was ready to focus on having my own relationship, and playing "I spy" was not my specialty, especially when it didn't have anything to do with me.

Nina was outside waiting for me when I pulled up. She was on the phone with somebody that had her grinning hard as hell. She waved at me but stayed on the phone for another couple of minutes before getting the car.

"Who had you cheesing so hard on phone?"

"Oh, I was talking to Jamal."

"Why didn't you get in the car instead of standing outside in the cold?"

"I needed a little privacy because Jamal wanted me to talk dirty to him. I'm sure you didn't want to hear all that."

"Nah, you did the right thing." I never pegged Jamal as the type of dude who got off on phone sex but then again I never thought he would be marrying an obvious hot box like Nina, either.

"I'm surprised we're going to the game. I could've sworn you said you don't date athletes," Nina said, jumping to the next subject.

"This isn't a date. I'm going to a basketball game wit' you."

"Yeah, you're going with me because dude that got you the tickets is playing in the game. If he wasn't you know I wouldn't be here right now."

"True dat. I can't front—he got my curiosity piqued 'cause even after all that shit went down last night in the club 'cause of Mike's crazy ass the nigga still called. I had to respect the fact that a little thing like guns blazing in front of his face did-n't make him want to forget my name and number. I guess all athletes aren't soft after all," I chuckled. "But enough about Jalen, pretty soon you'll be a married woman, how you feel 'bout that?"

"Excited, Jamal is such a wonderful man. He's so giving, and he truly adores me you know," Nina stated, making it clear it wasn't a question to be debated. "Speaking of my impending walk down the aisle, I wanted to ask you some-thing."

"What is it?"

"I know this may be a little awkward given your history with Jamal, but I would love if you would be one of my brides-maids." I glanced at Nina for a brief moment to see if she was serious. Her facial expression gave every indication that she was. I tapped my nails on the steering wheel deliberating my response.

"Nina, first let me clear something up for you. Jamal and I fucked a few times when we were teenagers. Yeah, I have a great deal of respect for him, but please spare me wit' this history shit like dude was my first love, broke my heart and now it's killing me to see him wit' you."

"I didn't mean it like that, Precious."

"Then why you throwing around words like *awkward* and *history?*"

"Honestly, I just didn't know how you would feel being in my wedding since you had slept with Jamal before, that's all."

"Shit, fuck it being awkward for me being in your wedding 'cause of my past dealing wit' Jamal, how 'bout I barely know you."

"Precious, I apologize. I've obviously gone about this all wrong. You're right; whatever you had with Jamal is irrelevant. Maybe the situation is awkward for me. I mean, look at you, you fly as hell and whether Jamal wants to admit it or not I'm sure he caught feelings for you. So maybe it's my own insecurity getting the best of me. But I have a lot of respect for you and I enjoy your company. I thought you enjoyed my company, too, but I guess I was wrong."

Nina's words seemed sincere, and I felt that maybe I came at her a little too harsh. Where I came from you never gave a chick the benefit of the doubt because they would disappoint you every time. I'd been thinking she was trying to say some slick undercut shit in regards to my past dealing with Jamal, but the truth was the shit was bothering her.

"I do enjoy hanging out wit' you, and I think you cool. And I would be honored to be one of your bridesmaids. Just don't have me in no ugly-ass dress." We both burst out laughing.

"Thank you, Precious. You have no idea how much this means to me. I'll have to find a way to repay you for coming through for me."

This was my second basketball game in less than a month, and I had to admit I was enjoying this shit. If you wanted to see any rapper or budding R&B princess, coming to a Knicks game would for sure guarantee that you would. Jigga Man and Beyoncé were front and center. Right beside them were Nas and Kelis. The more I looked around I wasn't sure if this was a basketball game or a hip hop convention. After getting an eyeful of the industry elite I focused my attention back on the court. Jalen had the ball and was dribbling down the court; he paused as if about to pass the ball but instead he did a slick crossover and seemed to fly in the air as he slam dunked the ball. The crowd went crazy over that shit, and so did I. As he hung on the rim the sight of every muscle in his body rippling was making my pussy wet. I hadn't fucked in so long, and his 6'4" sexy brown ass was exactly what I needed.

After the game Nina and I waited for Jalen to come out. Keith came out the locker room first, sporting the black eye he received courtesy of Mike. He gave me and Nina foul-ass stares.

"Girl, Keith look like he 'bout to come over here and beat us down," whispered Nina.

"He can play wit' his life if he want to."

"You not scared?" Nina asked in a serious tone. *Nina has no clue as to who I am. To be scared is to have no plan and I always have a plan—it consists of two shots to the head,* I thought to myself.

"Fuck 'im," were the only words I could muster for that cat. While we stood trying to ignore the heat Keith was throwing in our direction, Jalen stepped out looking finer than a motherfucker in a rich caramel colored two-piece suit. That nigga was looking the part of an NBA superstar, and I was dying to have all of him in between my legs.

"What's up, beautiful. I'm glad you came," Jalen said, giving me a kiss on the cheek. He nodded at Nina, and then Keith's punk ass came walking over to us.

"I figured it was you who invited them to the game," were the first words out of Keith's mouth.

"Damn, we can't get a hello or nothing," Nina said, trying to break the tension.

"How's that eye?" I asked, looking him straight in the face. I could care less about how that nigga felt. I wasn't about to kiss his chump ass. If he had kept his mouth shut at the club he wouldn't be walking around like he took a basketball to the face.

"So what you ladies tryna do, y'all want to get somethin' to eat?" Jalen asked, ignoring the negativity Keith was bringing.

"I thought you was leaving tonight?" I asked.

"Most of my teammates are, but we play in Philly tomorrow, so unless you got other plans I can hang out with you and leave in the morning."

"That works for me," I said with a smile. I knew exactly what I had planned for the two of us.

"If it's cool, I can stay, too and we can all go out to eat," Keith suggested. We all stared at him simultaneously. I was the first to snap out the trance and speak up.

"That's cool. Is it cool wit' you, Nina?" Nina nodded her head, going with the flow. I couldn't stand Keith's ass, but he could entertain Nina so she wouldn't feel like a third wheel with me and Jalen.

We headed out and decided to dine at Chin Chin on the East Side. Nina recommended the spot and none of us were disappointed. Their Chinese food was banging and tasted fresh. By the time we went through our second bottle of champagne I was ready to break out.

"How 'bout we leave here so we can have some privacy," I suggested to Jalen. Of course he put up no argument.

"Say the word and we out."

"Nina, I'm ready to head home. Do you want me to give you a ride?"

"I'll make sure she gets home," Keith volunteered.

"Is that cool wit' you, Nina? I don't have a problem dropping you off," I offered, as if I really cared.

"Thanks, Precious, but I'm good. I'll call you tomorrow." I was relieved like a motherfucker that Keith had stepped up. I only had one thing on my mind, and taking Nina home wasn't it.

By the time we got to Jalen's hotel room I had damn near taken off my clothes. Being backed up had sent my sexual desire into overdrive. I was dying for a nigga to twist my back out and Jalen did not let me down. He scooped me up and gently laid me down on the bed removing my remaining clothes. I closed my eyes as his tongue sucked my breasts and his fingers massaged my clit. At first I wanted him to start just pounding my pussy out because I hadn't had any dick in so long, but his foreplay felt so good it was getting me more open. The nigga had me grinding my hips as he finger fucked me. Then he stopped sucking my tits and popped my pussy with his tongue and fingers simultaneously. He had my legs spread wide open as I arched my back about to explode.

My juices flowed and Jalen licked them up as if it were his favorite drink. Then right when I thought it couldn't get no better, he reached for a Magnum XL condom, put it on and eased all ten inches inside of me. That shit had a bitch in pain for a second but it quickly turned to pleasure. I wrapped my legs around his back and he lifted my ass cheeks up so with every thrust, that nigga's dick felt like it was about to come out my throat.

I came at least three times that night, and it would've been more but after twisting me out for over two hours I finally had to put Jalen on pause. He had stamina like a stallion but a bitch was tired. Every time I would have an orgasm my energy would drain more and more, but it seemed to rejuvenate Jalen. When we finally chilled, I realized how much I missed falling asleep in the arms of a man.

When I woke up the next morning, Jalen was already in the shower. I knew he had to leave early to go to Philly, but I was hoping he could hit me off one more time before breaking out. I decided I would go to him, but before I was able to head to the bathroom there was a knock at the door. I assumed Jalen must have ordered some breakfast because a dude with all that height and build must stay hungry. I grabbed his T-shirt and put it on before answering the door.

"Who is it?" I asked, peeping through the hole.

"Room service," the gentleman replied. His face was looking down, but I could see he was holding a tray so I let him in. The moment I slightly opened the door, two men kicked it open barely giving me a chance to move back. I fell to the ground and one of the guys rushed me. He put his hand over my mouth and I tried to bite the shit, but the way he had it positioned I couldn't latch onto any skin. The other man, who was holding the tray, shut the door and pulled out his gun.

I figured these niggas somehow got word that a superstar athlete was staying in this room and decided to rob him. Both dudes were tall and big as shit. The one holding me down reached in a small bag he was carrying and pulled out some duct tape and rope. The nigga definitely knew what he was doing because he had me tied and taped up in less than sixty seconds. My mind was spinning trying to figure out what to do next. I wondered if Jalen could hear any of the commotion going on, but I seriously doubted it. I finally heard the water turn off. My heart was pounding so hard. It was becoming clear that this wasn't about a robbery because the niggas hadn't ransacked shit. After tying me up and placing me on the bed they just stood standing by the bathroom waiting patiently for Jalen to come out.

"What the fuck," Jalen barked when he opened the bathroom door and was greeted with the sight of me tied up on the bed. Jalen never even had a chance to make a move because one of the men used the butt of his gun to strike him on the side of his head. He did it with so much force I think it gave Jalen a minor concussion because his eyes rolled to the back of his head and he seemed to lose his balance. But if that first hit didn't take him under, the one that followed surely did.

The two men pounded on Jalen like he stole they last bag of dope. I felt so helpless as I watched them beat the shit out of him, and what made it worse was that I had no idea why. Besides feeling pity for Jalen, I feared that once the men finished him off they would rape and beat me. Being raped by a man had to be my worst nightmare. Without access to a knife or gun the men had all the power to have their way with me. My mind drifted back to the ass-whipping Jalen was receiving, and I realized that the moans I had heard from him at first had all but disappeared. I couldn't grasp that just last night this nigga had given me one of the best fucks of my life, and now I was watching him die.

Finally the punching and the kicking ceased and the men both stared at me. I closed my eyes for a minute thinking that I couldn't believe this was how I was going out. Being fucked and beat by some big black grimy niggas. I decided that if the opportunity presented itself, I wasn't going down without a fight. I was going to draw blood from one of those fuckers. I prepared myself to take whatever they was bringing and opened my eyes back up, but to my surprise they were gone. I was completely dumbfounded. I didn't know what this shit was about.

I tried to scoot my body over to the edge of the bed to see if Jalen was dead or alive. But I was wrapped up so tight

I could barely move. It was three hours before we were found, and that's because the maid finally came to clean the room. She screamed in Spanish for damn near five minutes before someone heard her cries and ran to the room and snapped her out of her daze. Soon after, the hotel security and police were everywhere.

When the duct tape was removed from my mouth I explained to the officers everything that went down. I watched as the paramedics tried to resuscitate Jalen, but it wasn't looking good for him. They carried him off and all I could do was shake my head in disbelief. I was beginning to feel like fucking with me was the kiss of death.

I was escorted to police headquarters although I had already told the cops everything I knew, but they still wanted to drill me. When we arrived they took me to a room that had one long table and two chairs. It was dreary and smelled of cigarettes, coffee and stale donuts. One of the detectives pulled the chair out for me as if trying to be polite.

"Mrs. Mills," the other detective, who was sitting across the table from me, spoke first, "I know you've had a rough morning, but I need you to look through some photos to see if you recognize your assailants. I stared intently at each picture but didn't see the two burly beasts who bum rushed the room and beat the shit out of Jalen.

"Nah, I don't see them."

"Look a little closer," he persisted. I did another look through and still didn't recognize them.

"They're not in here." The detective then shoved the book across the table at me hitting my chest.

"Yo, what the fuck is wrong wit' you? What, you hard of hearing? I said them motherfuckers not in here. And you pushing this book at me ain't gon' make my eyes see differently." I stood up out my chair. I was done talking to these disrespectful clowns, "Excuse me, I'm ready to go."

"You're not going anywhere until you answer our questions," the bug-eyed white detective stated firmly. "I believe you know much more than what you're telling us, and you won't be leaving until I get some answers."

"I told you everything I know, and this going in circles bullshit is working my very last nerve. I'm tired, and I want to go the fuck home."

"First, your husband, Supreme, and now Jalen Montgomery. One is dead; the other is knocking on death's door. What do they both have in common? You. Being in your presence is costing these men their lives, why is that?" The detective was playing hardball, and it was somewhat working. I had been asking myself the same shit. It was as if I was cursed, but I wasn't going to give this prick the satisfaction of knowing his question was wearing hard on my mind.

"Listen here, my man, that's what the NYPD gets paid for, to figure out crimes. So get on your job." Right when the detective looked at if he wanted to spit in my face, a short white man with glasses burst through the doors. Both of the detectives stared at him and then put their heads down as if disgusted.

"I hope you gentleman haven't been in here badgering my client because I would hate to have the two of you repri-manded, or even worse, sue this department."

"On what grounds?" the detective questioned.

"I'm sure I can come up with something. Now excuse me, my client will be leaving now." The attorney walked over to me and gently took my hand escorting me out.

"We're not done with you, Mrs. Mills," the detective said in a threatening tone.

"Yes, you are. If you have any questions please have them directed to my office. You know the number." I followed the attorney out the door with a sense of relief. I didn't know his name—I hadn't ever even seen him before, but I was grateful he got me out of that dark hole.

"Thanks for that, but who are you?" I asked, wanting to know how he popped up on the scene.

"Attorney Joseph Steinback. I was sent here by Mr. Owens."

"Mr. Owens?" I asked with confusion written on my face.

"Yes, Mike Owens."

"Oh, Mike, crazy me, I'm not used to hearing him addressed by his last name."

"I understand." He smiled.

"How did Mike know I was here?" But there was no need for Joseph Steinback to answer the question. The moment we exited the police headquarters, the paparazzi and news reporters swarmed me.

"Mrs. Mills, why were you in the hotel room with Jalen Montgomery?" one reporter yelled.

"Do you think Jalen will pull through, or will he die like your husband Supreme?" another barked.

"Mrs. Mills, did the men who tried to kill Jalen rape you?" I couldn't stomach another remark and neither could Joseph. He held my hand firmly and stopped dead in his tracks, looking each individual square in the face in turn.

"That is enough. My client will not be answering any of your tasteless questions. I would appreciate it if you all would step out of the way so we can get by." Joseph obviously garnered a certain level of respect because the cameras kept flashing, but they moved out of our way. The driver opened the door to the awaiting car and we drove off.

When we arrived back at my estate I noticed Mike's Aston Martin parked in the driveway. I was in no mood to see him but felt somewhat obligated since he retained Joseph Steinback on my behalf.

"Did you want to come in?" I asked Joseph when the car came to a stop.

"No, I'm sure you're exhausted. We can talk tomorrow.

But remember, don't speak to any reporters, and if the police come knocking call me immediately."

"Will do, thanks again." I walked to the door going over what I would say to Mike. Technically I didn't owe him an explanation but felt that I had to give him one. Before I even had a chance to get my thoughts together I saw a girl that looked no more than sixteen standing at the front as if waiting to greet me.

"Hi, Precious," she chirped, sounding extremely comfortable in my space.

"Who are you and why are you standing in my doorway?"

"Maya, girl, calm down and bring your ass inside," Mike said, reaching his hand out for me. "Precious, this is my sister Maya. She can be a bit forward." Seeing the two of them standing next to each other you couldn't help but see the resemblance. Maya inherited the same gorgeous genes as her brother, besides being a shade lighter and having long hair. Aside from that, they were the spitting image of one another.

"Don't worry about it. I just wasn't expecting to see her standing in front of my door."

"Wow, so you the girl that was married to Supreme and got to lay down next to him every night. That's what's up," Maya said, winking her eye at me. *Another grown-ass girl,* I thought to myself.

"We need to talk," Mike said seriously, ignoring his sister's comment.

"I'm sure, but where's Nathan?"

"They're out back. Some news media tried to sneak on the property. Nathan and the other security are keeping it under control." I started walking toward the library so Mike and I could talk. Maya was right behind us, I guess thinking she was going to sit in on the conversation, too. Of course Mike had to shut the door in her face so she'd realize it wasn't happening.

"I can't believe this shit," I said while pouring myself a drink.

"What did you expect, you got your face splashed across every station. What the fuck were you doing in Jalen's hotel room anyway?"

"I've been interrogated all morning and afternoon by the fuckin' cops—I don't need to come home and hear the same shit from you."

"If it wasn't for me you'd still be down there, so you need to be thanking me instead of poppin' shit."

"Thank you, but I got a lot on my mind right now. For one, I need to find out how Jalen is doing."

"Fuck Jalen. When are you going to comprehend that these little silly niggas ain't for you. I'm the only man that can take care of you right. Every time you get yourself caught up in some bullshit who is the one that makes it right?" I sipped on my drink taking in what Mike said. From disposing of that body to helping me understand the ins and outs of the music industry now that I owned the masters to Supreme's music, and then this, yeah, Mike always seemed to be right there when I needed him the most.

"I hear you. But what's up wit' your sister?" I knew my diversion from our initial conversation was going to piss him off, but my head was spinning and I needed a break from discussing that shit.

"I see what you're doing, but that's cool," Mike said, rubbing his hands together as if trying to calm his nerves. "My mom's having some problems wit' Maya and asked me to step in."

"Step in how, give her a lecture?" I asked sarcastically.

"A little more than that, she wants me to keep her for a couple of weeks."

"What about school?"

"That's the thing—she got suspended for ten days."

"For what?"

"Fighting and shit."

"How are you going to watch over your sister, you going to have her go to work with you every day?"

"That's the thing. I was hoping you could help me out." I damn near dropped my glass when I heard the word "help" come out Mike's mouth. I had a funny feeling that something was up as soon as I saw his sister greeting me at the door all cheerful.

"Yo, I feel for you, but there ain't nothing I can do to help with your sister. I got mad other shit going on."

"Yeah, like fuckin' wit' soft-ass basketball players."

"Here we go again." I poured myself another round wishing I was knocked out in my bed instead of going back and forth with Mike.

"Fine, I'll put it like this. Who got rid of that body for you?" I was glaring daggers at that nigga, mad that he even brought that shit up. "Listen," he continued, "I'm not asking you to baby-sit Maya 24/7, I'll drop her off on my way to work and pick her up when I get off. I'm asking for a favor, Precious."

Everything inside of me wanted to scream "no," but Mike had come through for me on more than one occasion. I would be dead wrong to shut him down. "How old is shorty, anyway?"

"Fifteen. She's really not a bad kid, just a little spoiled. With us growing up without our father I tried to step in and give her everything she wanted. I might've gave her too much. Besides my moms, she's all I have."

"I got you. I'll hold her down while you handle your business."

"I appreciate that, Precious. I hate to do this to you, but can you start today? I got this meeting I really need to get to."

"Is that the fuck why you had your attorney rushing down to the police station, 'cause you needed me to baby-sit?"

"Nah, I swear that's not why. I wanted you out," Mike said laughing. "But on the real, you need to stay away from that Jalen nigga. Didn't that beat down he received wise you up? He ain't for you." Mike kissed me on the cheek before walking out. Of course when he opened the door, Maya had obviously been listening to our conversation and jumped when her brother caught her.

"Oh, I was about to knock on the door," Maya said, trying to play it off.

"Whatever. Listen," Mike put his hand on Maya's shoulder, letting her know he was serious. "I have to head out to this meeting and Precious was nice enough to let you stay here with her." Maya locked eyes with me as her brother continued to talk. "I don't want you giving Precious no problems. You understand?" Maya nodded her head "yes" and gave Mike the puppy dog eyes, looking all angelic. "That's what's up. So I'll see you two ladies later on this evening. Thanks again, Precious."

"No problem." I walked Mike out, and as soon as I closed the door, Maya wasted no time.

"So, Precious, where we going, you tryin' to hit the mall or what?"

"No, I'm hitting the shower then going to bed. You need to go sit down and watch some music videos or something. But do not bother me, I'm tired as hell. If you need anything to eat, have Anna fix it for you."

"So, you just bailing on me? I thought you was cool, guess I wrong."

"Guess you was." I grabbed a couple of items and headed to my bedroom. I could feel Maya burning a hole in my back as I took my ass upstairs. But I was too tired to care. I did plan on spending some time with her, it just wasn't going to be that day.

Rules to the Game

I was so exhausted that by the time I woke up, it was the next day. The first person I thought about when I opened my eyes was Jalen, and then Maya immediately popped in my head. I didn't even say bye to her before she left, and Mike would be bringing her back over here any minute. I knew dealing with her was going to try my patience, but I already told Mike I would do it so I had no choice but to keep my word. Before I allowed myself to lose my train of thought, I picked up the phone and called the hospital where Jalen was.

"Good morning, Mount Sinai Medical Center," the operator chirped.

"Hi, can I please be connected to Jalen Montgomery's room?" There was a slight pause. I assumed the lady who answered the phone was checking for Jalen's information.

"I'm sorry, but this patient isn't accepting any calls," she informed me.

"Well, I'm his sister and would like to know how he's doing."

"What is your name?"

"Michelle Montgomery," I replied confidently as if the made up name was the truth. There was another pause, this time slightly longer.

"I'm sorry, but your name isn't on the patient's list. So I can't answer any of your questions."

"There must be some mistake. I just want to know how my brother is doing."

"Ma'am, I understand your concern, but I've been given strict instructions. There's nothing I can do for you." I wanted to reach through the phone and smack the lady, but there was no use in arguing with her. I sat in bed for a minute contemplating who could give me an update on Jalen's condition. I thought of someone who might be able to help me.

Ring...Ring...Ring

"Hello," Nina answered, sounding out of breath.

"Hey, girl, what's up?"

"Precious, how are you? I called you a few times yesterday but you didn't pick up."

"Yeah, I was really out of it."

"That's understandable. So what happened? They were talking about you and Jalen all day yesterday on the news, but nobody seemed to have the story straight."

"Nina, I promise to fill you in, but I'm not in the mood right now. Have you spoken to Keith?" I asked, jumping straight to the point.

"Yeah, I spoke to him yesterday."

"Did he tell you what kind of condition Jalen was in?"

"He's pretty bad, but he's going to pull through." I let out a deep sigh, relieved that Jalen would be okay.

"Did Keith say anything else?"

"Besides that you're bad luck and he warned Jalen to stay the fuck away from you, no, nothing else."

"Thanks for the info, but I gotta go now."

"Wait, don't forget my wedding is in less than two weeks. You're the only one who hasn't gotten fitted for your dress,"

Nina added before I had a chance to hang up the phone.

"Well, that's because you only asked me to be in the wedding two days ago."

"I know it was last minute but we still have to get it done."

"Fine, I'll call you later on to get the details. But I have to go now." This time I hung up the phone quickly, not letting Nina drop another word. I desperately wanted to go to the hospital to visit Jalen because in the pit of my stomach I felt responsible for what happened. I couldn't shake that feeling.

By the time I got dressed and went downstairs Maya was already there, sitting in the dining room eating breakfast. "Good morning," I greeted her, wanting to start the day on a good note.

"Hey," Maya replied dryly.

"I know yesterday I was in a bad mood, but I had just gone through some bullshit. I've got my rest so we're working on a brand new page. So let's try this again. Good morning," I said extra cheerfully.

"Good morning, Precious," Maya said, putting some pep in her voice. Whether it was sincere or not was irrelevant to me.

"That's better. Now, I have to run a few errands today, are you rolling wit' me or you staying here?"

"Ooh, I wanna roll wit' you."

"Cool."

"Precious," I heard Nathan call out from the other room.

"Nathan, I'm in the dining room."

"Jamal is here for you," he said, entering the dining room.

"Thanks, tell him I'll be right there."

"Dang, who Jamal, is he sweet on you?" Maya inquired.

"Excuse me?"

"Just asking. You know my brother digging you, and I was wondering if Jamal was his competition. But then maybe it's the basketball dude Jalen. That mess been all over the television and newspapers. You got a lot jumpin' off."

"I have to speak to Jamal, but mind yo' business and stay outta mine." With those departing words I went to handle things with Jamal.

"How are you feeling?" were the first words Jamal had for me as he followed me to the living room.

"I'm fine, Jalen is the one in the hospital not me. I'm assuming that's what you were referring to?"

"Yes. I had no idea the two of you were dating."

"We were in the beginning stages, but it's ended before it even had a chance to really begin."

"That's too bad, but I'm sure you'll find somebody," Jamal said sincerely.

"Enough about me, what brings you here?"

"I wanted to check up on you and ask about Nina. You know we're getting married next Saturday."

"I know—time flies. Can you believe I'm going to be one of the bridesmaids?"

"Yeah, when Nina told me you agreed to it I was shocked."

"It is your wedding, and Nina's not so bad."

"Does that mean you don't have any dirt to share with me?" he asked in a tone that seemed unsure of what the answer would be.

"Jamal, you can relax. Nina is harmless. She might flirt a little bit, but there's nobody else. She's in love with you." A smile broadened across Jamal's face, happy with my report.

"Thank you for doing this. I know you didn't want to spy on Nina. But I'm glad you put my paranoia to rest."

"Me too."

"I know you've got a lot on your mind, but I need to ask you about Supreme. Have you decided what you're going to do with his music?"

"I'm still figuring some things out. A couple of weeks ago I spoke to Mike about his thoughts since he owns Pristine Records. He's done very well for himself in this business, and

I wanted to get his opinion on how much I should ask for if I decided to sell."

"I can understand that. So what did he say?"

"He told me I shouldn't sell the music, but instead put it out myself."

"What do you mean, put it out independently?"

"Yeah, or seek distribution with a major label but still hold onto the rights. What do you think?"

"Of course you know I want Supreme's music for a lot of reasons. But speaking to you on a friendship level and not business, I would advise you to really do your research before jumping into the music industry. It's extremely cut-throat, and while it's wise to seek knowledge from Mike, I would also question what his motives are. I'm going to leave you with that food for thought, but you know I'm always here if you want to talk. If nothing comes up then I'll see you at my wedding." Jamal smiled.

"Of course." After showing Jamal out, I got my purse and told Maya to come on so I could run my errands. I listened to Jay-Z's "*Kingdom Come,*" rehashing all the bullshit that had been invading my life since Supreme's death. It was like a domino effect that wouldn't stop. I was so caught up in my thoughts that I didn't even hear my cell ring.

"Precious, here, your phone is ringing," I finally heard Maya say, snapping me out of my thoughts.

"Hello," I answered, still halfway zoning out until I recognized the voice on the other end of the phone.

"You still want that Nico information or what?"

"No doubt."

"A'ight, so meet me next Saturday at twelve o'clock. I'll call you earlier that day to let you know the spot."

"Next Saturday is no good for me, what about this Saturday?"

"Do you want Nico Carter or not?" she said defiantly, making it clear it was her way or no way.

"I'll be there."

"Smart decision, I'll be in touch." I didn't appreciate the way that bitch was carrying me, but my thirst for Nico was far stronger than my anger over her behavior. I preferred not to do the shit on the same day as Jamal's wedding, but if I met the chick at twelve then I still had a few of hours to make it back in time for a three o'clock starting time. It would be tight, but I couldn't miss what sounded like a real opportunity to finish Nico off. However, if I found out this bitch on the phone was wasting my time, then the same knife I planned to slit Nico's throat with would find its way to hers.

"Who was that?" Maya asked after I hung up the phone.

"I coulda swore I told you to stay out my business."

"That call seemed to get under your skin. I was concerned, that's all."

"Save your concern for somebody who needs it, I'm good."

"Damn, why you gotta be so hostile? I don't understand why we can't be friends." My neck actually snapped back due to that question.

"Friends? I'm almost twenty-one, how old are you?"

"Fifteen," Maya stated proudly.

"Girl, first of all I don't have friends, and if I did it wouldn't be wit' yo' young ass. What the hell do we have in common?"

"We both used to the ghetto fabulous life. You a baller chick and my brother got extra long paper, so I'm a baller chick, too. That's a start."

"Sweetheart, let me explain something to you. Your brother has given you everything you have, ain't nobody ever gave me shit. Do you know what I was doing when I was fifteen? Busting my ass working at a detailing shop tryna find a nigga to trick on me 'cause my moms wanted to pimp me out in the street. I lived the good life for this long," I said, snapping my finger. "Then it was all taken away from me when Supreme died. I learned to ball because I had no choice, and after getting a little taste of the streets it made me greedy. You, my dear, are trying to ball off your brother's loot. There's a big difference."

"What you mean? I got an older nigga that trick on me. He pushing keys and everything, so I ball off of more than just my brother's paper."

"Let me school you on something, youngin'. When you start fuckin' wit' them older hustlers in the streets, they not taking your young ass seriously. You just a pretty piece of pussy they want to have on they roster. They putting that real time in wit' them older bitches that got official jobs and good credit. Why? 'Cause they lacking that shit themselves. They know a lil' fifteen-year-old can't get no houses or apartments or cars in they name, so they hustling the older bitches who can.

"See, I always knew shit like that 'cause my man Boogie, may he rest in peace, hipped me to that shit. Unlike you, I didn't have no rich-ass family member hittin' me off wit' paper and whatever else I wanted. You fuckin' blessed and you wanna brag 'bout some hustler in the street breaking you off wit' chump change while you give up your most precious gift. 'Cause at the end of the day, if all else fails, your beauty and body is all you have. Don't sell yourself short, especially when you don't have to." After I said my piece I turned the music back up. I glanced over at Maya and noticed tears streaming down her cheeks. At first I wasn't going to say nothing, but then she started sniffling and I could tell she was all choked up. I reached in the glove compartment and handed her some tissues.

"Thank you," Maya said between sobs.

"It wasn't my intention to make you cry, but I had to keep it real wit' you, Maya. Life is too short to waste it on bullshit. I turned to the streets out of survival, and it made me cold. That doesn't have to be your life. With the type of money your brother has, you have the opportunity to be anything you want to be in this world. You can be so much more than a hustler's wife. That's a hood dream, baby, and you beyond that, and that's coming from a real bitch who know this game."

For the rest of our ride there was complete silence between us. When we arrived at the store on 52nd and Lexington Avenue, where I was getting fitted for my brides-maid's dress, Maya seemed to pull it together. Her eyes filled with amazement when we opened the glass double doors and entered the opulent store. The regal boutique was full of gowns from wispy sheer dresses to mermaid styles—most of them adorned with delicate beading and embellished embroidery. "Damn, I can't wait to get married," Maya beamed as we walked on the ivory marble floor, following what seemed to be the yellow brick road.

"Can I help you ladies?" a well preserved, tall white lady asked.

"Yes, I'm here to get fitted."

"For a wedding dress?"

"No, for a bridesmaid's dress, the actual bride is Nina."

"Oh yes, Nina. She's here now. Follow me to the back." We could tell when we were getting closer because it sound-ed as if we had arrived at a block party in Brooklyn instead of an upscale bridal store. I could hear Nina's voice but couldn't see her because my view was obscured by three women who had the type of asses and tits that would jiggle across your television screen. "Nina, your other bridesmaid is here," the saleslady said.

By the expression on their faces when they turned around, we had obviously caught them off guard. "Precious, hi, I almost forgot you were coming," Nina said, scooting by her friends.

"Sorry, I was running late, but I'm here now," I said as Nina gave me a hug.

"Nina, I'll go get Precious' dress so the tailor can get her fitted."

"Thanks," Nina said to the saleslady then turned her attention back to me and her friends. "Everybody, this is Precious and…" Nina paused glancing at Maya.

"This is Maya, Mike's sister."

"Nice to meet you, Maya."

"Hey, ladies," the three women said in unison.

"Wow, Nina, I had no idea we'd be having a party up in here." I glanced at the table next to the cream velvet couches and there were two opened bottles of champagne, glasses and strawberries dipped in chocolate.

"Girl, you know how I do. Why don't you let me pour you a glass?"

"No, thank you."

"I'll take some," Maya said, moving forward toward the table.

"I think not." I put my hand up, indicating to Maya not to go any further.

"Well, come sit down until they bring out your dress." I sized up the three women as we sat down. They had "hoochie" written all over their faces. Each had twenty pounds of weave in an array of colors to match their various complexions, which went from butterscotch to dark chocolate. All of them had cute faces, tiny waists and the words "thirsty for money" dripping from the sides of their mouths.

"I'm Talesha," the girl in the middle of the color spectrum said, extending her hand. Her claws were so long I thought they would sink into my skin. "This is Brittany and CoCo." She pointed to the other women.

"My fault, I was so caught I forgot to introduce you to my other bridesmaids," Nina said, sipping on her champagne. "Precious, you haven't said what you think of my dress."

"What dress, the one you got on?"

"Yeah, girl, this my wedding dress, what else would I be talking about?"

"My bad, I guess I was expecting something stark white, ivory or cream, but pale gold is nice." I tried to smile to cover up my dislike for her dress.

"I didn't want to follow the traditional route. I wanted to put my own spin on this shindig. I mean, this is the new color for wedding dresses anyway." The three musketeers gave her a high-five, cosigning on her wedding gown choice. The dress was actually very pretty in an over-the-top ballroom gown type way. It had incorporated jewels and pearls along the neck and draped down the back. Indeed, it was far from traditional and very edgy even for the most modern bride.

"You've definitely done that, but it's cool. You will no doubt stand out as the star of your wedding, as you should." I started wondering what type of hot mess of a dress she would have us in. I prayed it wouldn't be too far to the left. To my pleasant surprise my dress was more traditional and very lovely. It was a pretty stardust-colored silk A-line dress with an empire waist, chiffon halter and back cascade. "Very lovely."

"This is hot," Maya added.

"Damn, sure is. I can't wait to get married so I can pick out my wedding dress—it's going to be sick," Talesha popped.

"That's right, but you better make sure your groom's paper is right. 'Cause it cost paper to put on a fly-ass wedding. But Nina ain't got to worry 'bout that because she got rich-ass Jamal footing the bill," Brittney boasted.

I watched as Nina sat back carrying on with her girlfriends, sucking up their words of encouragement. While the tailor fitted my dress all I thought about was poor Jamal. He was so out of his league fucking with a *ho*-fessional like Nina. There was no doubt in my mind that Nina would pop out one baby for insurance purposes, and the moment she got her figure back she'd be leaving the little one with a nanny as she hit the streets with her hot-ass friends. The next chapter would be divorce court. Oh fucking well, that was Jamal's life. It would definitely be one to grow on.

I then stared over at Maya. I was still feeling bad about my trying to school her earlier, but I hoped she understood that I wasn't trying to bring her down, but instead, lift her up. The streets took my soul when I was fifteen and had a firm grip until I fell in love with Supreme. But when he died the part of me that truly learned to love died, too. The street life hadn't stolen Maya's innocence yet and I prayed it never would. By the way she was so enthralled in the hoochies' conversation, it might've already been too late. Only time would tell.

Make a Wish

I woke up on a beautiful Sunday morning with a deep sense of despair and didn't understand why. The sun was shining bright, but instead of opening my curtains and relishing the sunlight I pulled the silk comforter over my head wanting to be in darkness. I tried to go back to sleep but kept tossing and turning. Then it hit me as if getting swept away in the ocean by a strong current...it was my birthday. Today I was twenty-one—finally, officially legal. When Aaliyah sang in her angelic voice that "age ain't nothing but a number" she knew what was up. I had felt legal damn near all my life. Maneuvering through life's struggles and tragedies will age any person. You get to the point where no one can tell you a damn thing because you've seen too much with your own eyes, and the experiences have left you bitter and cold.

Here I was supposed to be celebrating a day that many anticipate for years and reaching an age I thought for so long was out of my reach. Being a hell-raiser in the streets would certainly almost always lead to either an early death or lockdown, but I had defeated the odds. I had achieved the material gains I had aspired for, but nothing else. I was alone. I had no one—not the child I was supposed to give birth to nor the man I should have spent the rest of my life with. It was moments like this that for a brief second I would be ready to end it all. But then my motivation for living would kick in…Nico Carter.

Every time I was ready to check out and join Supreme I would think about Nico. He was the one who gave me so much in life and then he took it all away. I would've much rather he ended my life than take Supreme. Here I was surrounded by wealth but deprived of what I needed the most…the love of my husband.

When I finally dragged myself out of bed I went in the closet and pulled out the box I had put a lot of Supreme's belongings in. It was some of his prized possessions that I couldn't dare part with but couldn't stomach looking at every day. The reminder was too painful, but today I wanted to embrace that pain. In the box was a rare mixtape that he cut when he was still an underground artist and a press kit released by Atomic Records promoting his first solo debut including an 8x10 black and white photo and a five-page information packet printed on stationary from Atomic Records with a little about the CD explaining what each song is about and why he wrote it. There was also a platinum diamond-encrusted "Supreme 4 Life" pendant he received from the label when his debut CD went platinum.

But my favorite piece of memorabilia was Supreme's notebook filled with handwritten lyrics and poetry. Supreme would always tell me that he had memorized every rhyme he ever spit and had no need to write them down but chose to because one day he wanted to share his thoughts on paper for the rest of the world to read. I spent the next few hours in the closet laughing, crying and most importantly, reminiscing. In my time of deep thought I couldn't help but wonder what I would do after I had finally achieved retribution against Nico. What direction would my life lead me in? My mind had been so preoccupied with revenge that I hadn't looked toward the future. I guess I didn't see a future without Supreme in it, but maybe it was time for me to realize that I should. Supreme wouldn't want me to stop living because of the cards life had dealt me. He was a survivor and would want me to be a soldier.

I stepped in the shower and let the hot water baptize my body. I would handle my business with Nico and then put the misery of my past behind me and see what the world had to offer. I knew I would never share a love greater than the one I had with Supreme, but I had to try to figure out a way to live instead of just existing.

After I got out the shower I put on a cream Juicy Couture jogging suit and headed downstairs. Before I reached the bottom stair the doorbell rang. "Who the fuck is at my door on a Sunday afternoon?" I said out loud. Annoyed, I opened the door.

"Surprise! Happy birthday!" Jamal and Nina said in unison. They had balloons, cake, champagne and food.

"How did you guys know it was my birthday?"

Nina started excitedly, "A couple of weeks ago when we went out you left your wallet open on the table for a brief moment when you took a call on your cell phone, so I peeked at your license. I realized your birthday was coming up, and I thought it would be great to surprise you with an intimate party especially since you agreed to be in my wedding." My first instinct was to think back as to when I left my wallet open since that was out of my character. I didn't want to spoil the kind gesture, so I let it slide. "Are you going to keep us standing out here? This cake is getting heavy. Come on, Precious, let us in?" Nina asked.

"Yeah, Precious, I don't know how much longer I can carry this stuff," Jamal added.

"Sorry, come on in. I'm still a little surprised that you all showed up on my birthday."

"I hope you don't mind?" Jamal asked.

"No, it's a much needed surprise. It's either this or mope around the house all day."

"Well, we can't have you doing that. You're part of my clique now, and no girlfriend of mine is left to mope."

"Nina, that's sweet of you, but I'm not really the clique type."

"Now you are. Now let's go get this party started." Before we could get to the kitchen, the doorbell rang again.

"Did you all have somebody else with you?" Nina and Jamal looked at each other and then shook their heads. "Then who could it be?" I went to the door and found another surprise.

"Happy birthday, pretty girl," Mike said with a beautiful flower arrangement in one hand and a bottle of champagne in the other.

"Did someone put out a special service announcement that today's my birthday?"

"If they did, I didn't get it, but I don't need to. I know everything. By the way where are Nathan and the rest of the security?" Mike kissed me on the check and looked around the foyer, waiting for me to let him pass.

"It's Sunday, and I gave them the afternoon off to spend some time with their families. They'll be back this evening, and Anna will be back in the morning. Speaking of family, where is Maya?"

"I wanted us to celebrate your birthday alone, so I let her hang out with one of her girlfriends."

"I hate to burst your bubble, but we're not alone." Mike stepped inside only to see Jamal and Nina, who gave him a half-assed smile. "You're more than welcome to stay for the party. Two bottles of champagne is always better than one," I said taking the bubbly out of Mike's hand and the flowers.

"The flowers are gorgeous."

"Just like the birthday girl."

"You and Jamal go have a seat while Nina and I prepare the food and pour the drinks." The fellas nodded their heads, though neither one seemed enthused about their time alone. Nina and I headed to the kitchen and the questions kicked in immediately.

"So are you and Mike getting serious? I mean, him showing up trying to be alone with you on your birthday. He seem smitten to me."

"Mike is cool, but we haven't gone any further than being just friends."

"Do you think if Jamal and I hadn't showed up today that maybe it would've?" I eyed Nina.

"I don't think I understand your question."

"Don't be sly with me, Precious Cummings. You understand my question. If you and Mike were alone today on your birthday do you think you guys would have taken your relationship to the next level?" I remained silent putting the Jamaican food on the plates and opening the champagne. "Damn, let me say it in layman's terms: would you and Mike be having buckwild passionate sex tonight if you were alone?"

"You over there feenin' for the inside scoop, but I have none to give. Like I said, Mike and I are cool...period. Now grab those two plates, I'm ready to eat."

"Before we go, can I ask you one last question?" Nina's tone sounded serious. I decided to throw her a bone since they brought over some treats for my birthday.

"What is it?"

"Have you ever loved anyone else besides Supreme?"

"Why would you ask me that?"

"Just curious...I'm about to be a married woman and wondered if he would be my first and final love."

"So Jamal is the only man you've ever loved?"

"Yes."

I seriously doubted that, but then again Nina didn't really come across as the falling in love type. "Interesting. Honestly, I loved one other man."

"Who?"

"Nico Carter."

"The man Jamal said tried to kill you?"

"That's him. But hey, we can never choose who we'll fall in love with. Now enough questions, let's go eat." When Nina and I came out the kitchen we could hear raised voices. When we reached the dining room Jamal and Mike were standing practically toe-to-toe. "What is going on in here?" Both of the men turned to look at me.

"Oh, it's nothing. Jamal and I was just discussing business."

"It must have been awfully intense, since your voices were rather loud."

"I apologize, Precious. Mike and I had a difference of opinion with what you should do about Supreme's music."

"Do we really have to discuss this on my birthday?"

"Of course not, today is about you. Everything else is irrelevant." Mike came over and took the plates from my hands and put them on the table. I noticed Jamal giving him the look of death. I was tempted to ask Jamal to replay their conversation in it's entirety, but I wanted to spend a couple of hours not focusing all my energy on Supreme. He occupied my every thought for the majority of each day and night; my brain and heart needed a break.

"Cool, because if only for the duration of the afternoon I want us to enjoy each other's company."

"Whatever your heart desires," Mike said, being all extra. We all sat down and tore up the food. Then Nina brought out the cake she ordered from Make My Cake in Harlem.

"Precious, you have to make a wish before you blow out the candles," Nina said. I closed my eyes and wished for

Supreme's killer to burn in hell then blew out the candles, not missing one. They all applauded.

"What did you wish for?" Mike inquired.

"If I tell you that, then it won't come true."

When it came time for me to make a toast, I was actually enjoying myself. We all lifted our glasses and I looked at the three guests who I considered the closest things I had to friends. "I want to thank each of you for making this a wonderful birthday. When I woke up this morning I wanted this day to be over before it even started, but you all made it into something special. For that I'm grateful."

When the party came to an end I almost wasn't ready for it to end...almost. I showed all three to the door and watched as they walked to their cars. "Nina, I'll be right back, I forgot something," I heard Jamal say. He jogged back up to the front door as Nina and Mike continued walking.

"What did you forget, Jamal?"

"I just said that so it wouldn't look suspicious, me coming back up to speak to you," he whispered as soon as he reached me.

"What is it?"

"I don't mean to bring any negativity on your birthday, but I care about you, Precious, and I wouldn't be able to sleep tonight without telling you this."

"Telling me what?"

"Be careful with Mike."

"What did he say to you?"

"It's not what he said; it's how he said it. He's dangerous, that I know. So just be careful. I have to go but we'll talk later."

That night I went to bed replaying what Jamal said. There was an underlying tone of fear in his voice. The eye contact he made with me when speaking of Mike was powerful. I already knew Mike was a dangerous man, but Jamal sounded as if he had established that Mike was not only dangerous but deadly.

One Murder at a Time

Before I knew it, Saturday rolled around, and I woke up feeling anxious. As promised, the mysterious informant kept her word and called letting me know where to meet her, which turned out to be the city. Since the wedding was taking place at The Plaza Hotel, that was convenient.

As I got dressed I didn't know what to expect from the woman I was meeting. Hell, I wasn't sure a woman would even show up. She could've been a decoy for a big ruthless nigga—that's why I was going prepared with two nine millimeters and a knife. When I got downstairs, to my surprise and annoyance, Maya was sitting in the living room.

"Maya, what are you doing here?"

"You told Mike that I could go to the wedding with you, remember?"

"Yeah, I told him to drop you off at The Plaza at three, so why are you here and it's only ten?"

"He had to go out of town and wasn't going to be able to drop me off in the city at three. So he told me to chill at your place and ride to the wedding wit' you."

Just like a nigga, always putting they responsibilities off on the next bitch like we ain't got shit to do but baby-sit. How the fuck was I gonna manage this? I couldn't have Maya all up in the mix 'cause I didn't know what might go down. *I could drop her off at the hotel but then her hot ass might start turning tricks in there. She'll be better off just sitting in the car, at least I'll know where she is and that she's safe*, I thought.

"A'ight, get yo' shit. But don't ask me no questions and stay in the fuckin' car at all times unless I tell you otherwise. Understand?"

"Yes, I understand."

The first stop I made was to my storage spot. After all this time I still kept it. I didn't trust keeping my stash cash in my crib because too many people be coming through there. If my money came up short or missing it could be anyone from the security to the hired help. I didn't have time for those guessing games. I knew I was the only one with a key to this spot, so if some shit was amiss, that was on me.

I ran inside with a small duffel bag and got the one hundred thousand the girl asked me for. It was a far cry from the million I had floating in the street, but if the informant didn't know about it, who was I to tell?

After retrieving the money it was time for me to head to the city. Driving from my crib to the storage facility took me over an hour and I didn't want to be late for my twelve o'clock appointment. The closer I got to the city, the more I started feeling nauseous. I hoped it was jitters from being in the wedding and not an omen of my fate.

Right when I pulled out the Lincoln Tunnel I heard the chiming of my cell. "Yo," I answered. I knew it had to be homegirl since she had been the only one calling me from a blocked number.

"You got everything?" she stated sounding anxious. I figured she was referring to the money.

"Right here."

"Okay, meet me on 42nd and 9th."

"The bus terminal by Times Square, it's gon' be mad motherfuckers over there."

"I know. I'll call you in ten minutes and let you know where to give me the money."

"So we're clear, I'm not giving you shit until you give up the exact facts."

"I got you."

"Long as we on the same page. I'll be waiting for your call." Since I took the Lincoln Tunnel I was right by 42nd and 9th. I pulled my car on the corner block where I had a prime view of the street but was also discreet. If possible I wanted to figure out who the informant was before we met. With the block not being as crowded as I thought it would be, there was a good chance of seeing her. I sat there with the radio off in pure silence scanning the area like a hawk.

"Who you looking for?" Maya asked, letting her curiosity get the best of her.

"What I tell you before we left? In case you don't remember, I'll remind you. Sit there and don't ask me no questions. Ain't nothin' changed." Maya started fidgeting in her seat, and I knew she was dying to play twenty questions, but I wasn't having it. Just then my cell started ringing and it was coming from a blocked number. I stared extra hard seeing if I could peep anyone using their cell trying to call someone. In those few seconds I noticed five people on their cell—two middle-aged white men, a young Hispanic boy, an older black man and a black woman, who looked to be in her mid-twenties. I purposely didn't answer my phone to see which one would try to make the call again. My phone kept ringing as I tapped my fingernails, eyeing their moves.

"You not gonna answer your phone?" Maya asked, crossing her arms like she had an attitude. I turned and gave her the look of death so she knew I meant business and would leave her hard-headed ass sitting right on the curb. I quickly gave my attention back to the agenda at hand. I peeped mouth movement from three out of the five people I was watching, which meant they made contact, so I scratched them off the list. The two left were the Hispanic boy and the black woman. My phone stopped ringing and then it started again from the blocked number. I looked up to see which of the two was on their phone, and it was the black woman. This time I answered.

"Yo, what's up?"

"Why didn't you answer your phone a minute ago, I was about to leave."

"I doubt that, especially since you want your money." I watched from a short distance as the black woman I scoped out yapped on the phone talking to me. Homegirl was definitely a rookie at this because her game wasn't tight at all. She was actually on 42nd and 9th waiting for me like she said she would. A semi-pro would've held tight to see me in the spot first and watched from a distance to scan my moves before stepping on the scene, but she bypassed all that.

"Anyway, here's how it's going down. There is a telephone booth right at the corner on 9th. Right beside it is a trash can. Leave the bag with the money next to the trash can. Under the phone there is an envelope taped with all the information you need to get to Nico."

"Information like what?"

"The address to where Nico is staying."

"How I know this shit official?"

"You don't, but I'm telling you it is. It's up to you, so what you want to do?"

"Let's do this." I hung up the phone and noticed the girl disappear into a deli near the drop-off location. Then I turned to Maya. Homegirl might've been telling the truth but this shit was too important to gamble on. I needed to sit the bitch down and get to the bottom of some things.

"Maya, you always wanna be so down, I got a task for you that can earn you some stripes." Maya's eyes lit up real bright.

"What is it?"

"First, twist your hair in a bun. I want you to put on my baseball cap," I directed as I took off my hat. Luckily Maya and I were about the same complexion and basically the same build. With the hat on, no one could tell for sure if it was me or not, assuming that the woman knew what I looked like. Maya did what I asked and began getting excited at the thought of being down with my scheme.

"Now what, Precious?"

"Take this bag and drop it right next to that garbage can right there," I said, pointing to the corner where the trash can was. But before you do so make sure you get the envelope from underneath the phone in the phone booth. Do you understand?" I asked slowly and precisely.

"Yes. Get the envelope from under the phone and then leave this duffel bag next to the trash can," she repeated.

"Exactly. When you're done I want you to wait for me in that drug store across the street. You got your cell?" Maya nodded her head. "Okay, I'll call you when it's time for you to come out the store. It's imperative that you follow my exact instructions."

"I promise I won't let you down." I watched as Maya walked across the street with the duffel bag in tow. She went directly to the phone booth, patted her hand under the phone and ripped off the envelope. She then dropped the bag next to the trash and proceeded toward the drug store as instructed. With Maya in place, I slowly drove my car directly across the street so that the trashcan was on my left hand side. I eagerly waited for the woman to come out because I was positioned much closer to where the bag was located and would retrieve it before she ever had a chance. I already had my nine millimeter resting underneath a jacket and the second I noticed the woman walking toward the trashcan I swung into action. I reached the duffel bag in what seemed to be one leap.

"Excuse me miss, that's mine," she screamed out, not realizing who I was. We were now face-to-face, and before she could say another word or run for safety, I had my piece rubbed up against her ribs.

"Now I can either drop you right hear on 42nd Street or you can take a ride wit' me. It's up to you. The woman's whole body was shaking—this must have been the first time she ever felt steel that shot bullets.

"Please don't shoot me," she said with her voice trembling.

"I guess that means you'll take that ride wit' me. I'm sure you can drive so get in the driver's seat."

"I'm not really comfortable driving a Range Rover."

"Well, bitch, get comfortable, 'cause you only working wit' two choices: drive or die." As the woman started up the truck I kept the gun to her side as I called Maya.

"Hi, Precious, how did I do?" Maya asked with a sound of pride in her voice.

"Excellent. You still got that envelope?"

"Yes, it's right here in my hands. Can I open it?"

"No! Can you stay there for about ten more minutes?"

"Yeah, that's no problem."

"Good, I'll call you back shortly."

"I could've sworn I saw you drop off the duffel bag and take the envelope," said the girl with tears streaming down her face. "I even waited a few minutes and watched you leave."

"Nah, your eyes were playing tricks on you, but this gun is the real deal. Now pull right over there in that abandoned parking lot."

"Are you going to kill me?"

"That's up to you. I definitely don't have a problem killing you, but it depends if you gonna answer my questions truth-fully or if you're gonna lie."

"What do you want to know?" The high-yellow heifer had sweat beads coating her forehead. She couldn't even hide her fear.

"Who the fuck gave you my number, and who the fuck sent you after me? Answer those questions, and you might have a chance of seeing another day." The girl swallowed real hard. She didn't look no older than twenty, and I wondered how she got involved in this bullshit. I could still smell the Similac on her breath.

"Listen to me. I'm about to tell you the truth," she said, twisting in her seat as she prepared to spit her story. "This girl that I'm cool with called me like a few weeks ago asking me did I want to make some easy money. And of course I was down for it 'cause I'm in school, and I do little bullshit videos and stuff on the side to make a couple of dollars. So I was like, as long as I don't end up in jail or dead I'm down for whatever." The girl then looked down eying my gun as if pleading, *please don't kill me.* "So the girl promised me that the job was really easy. All I had to do was call this chick up say x, y and z, collect some money and I'm good."

"Yo, your story sound like some bullshit."

"I swear, look in my purse and you'll see the notes she gave me." I kept my gun purposely aimed at the girl and grabbed her purse that was sitting on her lap. "There it is, right there," she gestured with her finger pointing to a mani-la envelope. I opened it and saw what appeared to be a high-ly specific script. It even had the comment Nico made in ref-erence to death before he shot me. I studied every word on the script looking for a clue.

"I don't see anything on here about how much money you were supposed to ask me for in order to get the information on Nico."

"She never gave me one. That's why the first time I spoke

to you I had to cut our conversation short because I wanted to find out what amount of money to say. The girl told me to ask for whatever I wanted because more than likely you would pay, plus she said your paper was like that. She did tell me to ask you for a cute amount and give her twenty-five percent since she put me on. The deal I made with you was going to pay for my tuition, and I wouldn't have to do videos no damn more. I get tired of having to fuck bum-ass rappers and their boys all the time. I couldn't believe when you agreed to the amount, but now I see why you planned on snatching me up regardless."

"So did the girl show you a picture of me?"

"Nope."

"Did she tell you who she was working for?"

"Nope, she kept everything real simple. It's like a bunch of us that all run in the video girl circuit, and she was just putting me on to some quick dough."

"What's her name?"

"Whose name?"

"Bitch, the chick that set this shit up."

"Oh, *her* name? LeeLee."

"What was the next move you were supposed to make after I picked up the envelope and you got the money?"

"She told me to call her and let her know you picked up the envelope and I got the money; that was it."

"Well, then that's what you gonna do. What's yo' name, ma?"

"Vita."

"A'ight, here," I said, handing Vita her phone. "Call that chick LeeLee and tell her that I must've changed my mind 'cause I never showed up. Tell her you've been waiting for over an hour and when you tried to call me I didn't pick up my phone. You understand?"

"Yeah," Vita nodded her head.

"But yo, don't play no clue games wit' your homegirl.

'Cause sweetheart, I would hate to have your brains splattered in my Range Rover, but if that's what has to be done then so be it."

"No, I won't try nothing, I-I-I promise," Vita stuttered. "If I knew it was going to be all this drama I would've said forget it."

"What type of shit did you think you were being a part of when you were calling me demanding money and throwing faulty shit around about a nigga that tried to kill me?" I questioned.

"Honestly, I didn't want to know. Some easy money was the only thing on my mind."

"Huh, I guess nobody schooled you that all money ain't good money. Now make that call." As Vita dialed LeeLee's number I unzipped a bag full of goodies I had brought for the mission. I listened intently as Vita let her friend know the deal never went down. I could hear the frustration in the girl's voice as she asked Vita a million questions. Finally, I motioned my hand letting her know to wrap up the conversation. When she hung up I made my next move.

"Are you going to let me go now?" a naïve Vita asked.

"Do you know what information is in that envelope my partner picked up?" I said, ignoring the bogus question she hit me with.

"I assume the address to where the guy, Nico, is. I already told you that." *I hope it is the correct address because it's nothing like the element of surprise. If Nico and whoever is helping him thinks I never picked up the envelope then they won't be expecting me to show up. Fucked up for them, but great for me,* I thought to myself.

"Just checking, making sure your story is legit. Now put your hands behind your back." Vita looked down strangely at the handcuffs I was holding. "What, you ain't neva seen no handcuffs before?"

"Why you want me to put these on?" I chuckled for a

minute wondering why dumb broads get themselves involved in shit that's way out they league. She was playing with her life over greed, and she wasn't even a warrior.

"Vita, don't ask me no questions. Just make things easier on yourself and do as I say," I told her calmly.

"Are you going to kill me?" Her eyes were filled with tears and fear.

"If I wanted you dead you would be. So just cooperate and we good." She breathed a sigh of relief and hurriedly complied with my request. I then pulled out my duct tape and covered her mouth. I pushed the backseats down and told her to crawl to the trunk. As she lay with her feet facing me, I tied her legs up. Without saying a word I used the butt of my gun to pound Vita in the back of her head, and she was out like a light. I hoped she would remain unconscious until I finished handling my business. I covered her up with blankets and pushed the seats back up.

My next stop was to scoop Maya up. I called her and right when I pulled up to the drug store she came outside. "Is everything cool?" she asked after closing the door.

"Yeah, you did real good. Now let me have that envelope." Maya pulled the envelope out of her pocket and I ripped it open. Nico's name was written at the top with an address underneath. I knew this had to be a set-up. They were expecting me to drop the money, pick up the envelope, go to the address and then be ambushed. The shit might've worked if I hadn't snatched up Vita, but now I hoped that I had turned the tables and that I would ambush they asses.

I pulled up to the address on the paper, and I couldn't help but think the area seemed so familiar. I didn't come to Chelsea often, but I knew I had been in this area recently. I looked around trying to see a landmark but then my cell rang bringing me out of my thoughts. I saw that it was Jamal calling. I eyed the clock and realized it was two o'clock.

"Hi, Jamal," I said with ease.

"Precious, where are you and where is Nina?"

"Nina? She hasn't gotten to the hotel yet?"

"No, I figured she was with you. She's not picking up her phone and nobody seems to know where she is."

"No, Nina isn't with me. I got caught up in some drama with Mike's little sister, and now I'm stuck in traffic, but I should be there shortly. Nina probably left her phone someplace and is stuck in traffic, too. When's the last time you spoke to her?"

"Last night before she left to stay at one of her girlfriends' houses. She didn't want me to see her again until she walked down the aisle."

"Jamal, I'm sure Nina will be there any minute. There's nothing that can keep her from marrying you. Just hold tight, I'll be there shortly."

"You're right, but hurry up, I want you to be here," Jamal said, sounding much calmer.

"I will." I glanced at Maya and she was giving me the lips poked out look.

"What?" I asked Maya after hanging up with Jamal.

"'Some drama came up with Mike's sister.' How you gon' blame your tardiness on me?"

"You claim you wanna be down, so let's call you taking the blame on that earning your stripes."

"Well, if you put it like that, I'm cool," Maya said, smacking her lips like she was 'bout it, 'bout it. I refocused on my surroundings. I was parked a few buildings down from the address on the paper. I was checking to see if any familiar faces went in or came out, mainly Nico's. I wasn't expecting to see him, but then again anything was possible. I eyed the clock again and time was definitely not on my side. If Nico was in there then I needed to handle my business and be out.

"Maya, I want you to sit tight. I have to run up in that building, and hopefully I won't be gone too long. If an emergency comes up, call my cell. If I don't pick up, here." I handed her two hundred dollars. "Take a cab over to the hotel where the wedding is, but no matter what, don't tell nobody about what went down this afternoon. If anybody asks, just say I dropped you off at the hotel and said I'd be back shortly. You understand?"

"I understand, but you are coming back, right?" She reached over and gave me a hug. My eyes locked with Maya's and I saw traces of panic and genuine concern.

"Don't worry, Maya, I'll be fine. Just follow my lead." Honestly I wasn't sure if I would be fine because I didn't know what was waiting for me. All I knew was that I wasn't going to miss the opportunity to come face-to-face with Nico Carter. I wanted to bring this chapter of my life to an end. If I didn't avenge Supreme's death I could never move on. Nico was a hold up and he had to go—there was no other way around it. "Give me back the hat," I told Maya. She handed over the black baseball cap and I twisted my hair up in a bun.

"Be careful," Maya hollered before I shut the door. I walked briskly toward the building and to my relief a man was about to go in. Finding someone to buzz me in was one obstacle I didn't have to encounter. On my way in I quickly searched the buzzer for the Super's name and apartment number. I peeped that there was no name next to the apartment number Nico was supposedly staying at.

I knocked on the door, praying that the Super would answer. "Mr. Sanchez, are you there?" I heard a television and a dog barking. A few seconds later a petite Hispanic lady opened the door with a little terrier right by her side. She had to be the Super's wife. First she just stared at me not saying a word. "Do you speak English?" She nodded her head "yes," but still didn't say a word. "I need your help." I used the sweetest and most sincere voice I could muster.

"Help?" Mrs. Sanchez questioned in a thick Spanish accent. I could tell she was no pushover and I would have to give a very convincing story to get what I needed from her.

"Yes, last night I got in a huge argument with my boyfriend, and before he left he stole a watch my father left me before he died. I called the police, but after speaking to him they said there was nothing they could do because my boyfriend denied it, and it was my word against his. I know that watch is in his apartment, and I desperately need it back. That watch is all I have left from my father. Not only did he break my heart by cheating on me with my best friend, but now he has my dead father's watch." I let a tear roll down my cheek for special effect hoping that would evoke a twinge of sympathy. I studied the older lady's face, and I could see I was somewhat reaching her.

"What can I do?" She put her hands up as if confused.

"Let me in his apartment so I can get my father's watch. My boyfriend went out of town this morning, so he's not home. He'll never know. I promise I won't be in there long." The lady's eyes got extra big and her head switched back and forth as if stunned.

"Are you crazy? I can't let you in someone else apartment. Dat's against the law." I lowered my hands motioning for her to calm down. She was now talking loudly, and I didn't need to raise any suspicion.

"Listen, no one would have to know. He's not home. All you have to do is give me the key, and I'll be in and out. I promise it will be worth your while." I finally struck a chord with the lady. She lifted her eyebrow waiting to hear what I was offering. I pulled out a knot of money, full of nothing but Benjamin Franklins.

"What apartment is he in?" she asked in a much more cooperative tone.

"7E."

"Oh, yes, I do see a young lady visit him often. He don't leave apartment that much only very late at night. Must be when he come see you. He two-timer, what a shame, tsk,

tsk, tsk..."

"Yes, two-timer. He was living with me and seeing my best friend."

"What a shame. You deserve your father's watch back," Mrs. Sanchez continued now with her hand out as if every word she spoke cost me money. I started dropping one bill after another in the palm of her hand. When I hit five I stopped. "No key, no father watch." I gave her five more, and she rolled up the grand and tucked it in her bra. Then she pulled a bunch of keys from her bathrobe pocket. "You get caught, I say you robbed me for key, then you go to jail." She wiped her hands. "I have nothing to do with this. I don't know what you're doing, I've never seen you before," she said with her eyes closed as if I had miraculously disappeared and she hadn't handed over the apartment key. I said nothing—I had what I needed. I was also happy I had my baseball cap pulled down real low over my face so if shit hit the fan she wouldn't be able to give the police an accurate description of me. She closed the door as if nothing happened.

As I walked quietly up all seven flights of stairs I slipped on my gloves. My heart was beating so fast. I didn't know if it was an adrenaline rush from bring so close to ending Nico's life once and for all or anticipating the unexpected. When I reached his floor I put my ear to the door to see if I could hear anything, but there was complete silence. I discreetly pulled out my gun as I slowly opened the door with the key Mrs. Sanchez gave me. With it slightly open I used one eye to scan the open area. No one was in view, so I took my chances and went straight in with gun raised.

I could hear what sounded like the shower running. After closing the door I glanced around looking for clues that Nico was in fact staying here. The place was decorated decent enough with coffee colored leather furniture, a throw rug and a few plants, nothing spectacular, but respectable. I made a beeline to the bedroom, and I instantly knew that this was the place Nico was laying his head every night. He still wore the same cologne and the aroma filled the room. For a moment it brought back memories of how good he used to feel inside of me. Hearing the water stop snapped me out of my daydreaming.

I hurriedly tip-toed out of the bedroom and hid inside a hallway closet. I kept the door cracked open and watched as Nico came out the bathroom. He was butt naked and his smooth chocolate skin was glistening, highlighting every muscle on his solid frame. He had let his short, curly hair grow out and was now sporting cornrows. Part of me wanted to fuck him one more time before I had to lullabye his ass, but that was a bad idea. I stood patiently in the closet as I saw him walking back and forth from the bedroom to the bathroom getting dressed. When he was done he went in the living room, turned on the television and sat down. I waited about five more minutes so he could get comfortable and then sneaked up on him.

"Long time no see," I said, sneaking up on Nico with my nine millimeter pointing directly at his head. His dark eyes remained fixed on mine and he didn't flinch even with death staring him in the face.

"My lovely, Precious. I knew we'd meet again."

"I'm sure you did, just not under these circumstances."

"What do you mean by that?"

"Save the bullshit, Nico. I know you and some bitch named LeeLee was tryna set me up. You thought I was gonna show up here so the two of you could ambush me, but I stopped all that."

"Yo, on the real I don't know what the fuck you talking 'bout. I had no clue you was going to show up here. You think I would be chillin' on the couch watching TV waiting for you to put a bullet in my heard? You know me better than that."

"Actually I don't, because not in my worst nightmare did I believe you would come back and kill my husband. I understand you seeking revenge on me and tryna end my life because I tried to end yours first by setting you up on that murder charge. I'll take that as settling the score, even though because of your actions I also lost my unborn child. That was foul. But then you come back and blaze Supreme while we leaving the hospital. For that you gotta die."

Nico let out a deep sigh and shook his head. He put his hands over his mouth and rubbed his chin as if thinking. I stepped back a little bit while keeping my finger firmly on the trigger. I didn't know if the nigga would try to get slick and jump at me, trying to take my weapon. He was much more powerful than me, and I had to keep the upper hand at all times.

"We've both done some fucked up shit to one another, but I swear on everything I've ever loved, which includes you, I ain't kill Supreme. And honestly, when you said you were pregnant I didn't believe you. I thought you were trying to manipulate the situation and make me pity you so I wouldn't finish you off. I'm sorry I took the life of your unborn child, but I swear that I didn't kill Supreme. That's my word." I felt a slight pain in my heart. Nico spoke each word so clearly and defiantly. I knew this man on many levels, and it scared me because part of me believed he was telling the truth.

"You a fuckin' lie. Don't try to snake your way out this shit. You the only person that had reason and is crazy enough to come at Supreme in broad daylight. I know it was you."

"In your heart if you really believe I was the one, then go 'head and pull that trigger, go 'head," Nico pressed on. I stepped forward and gripped the gun tighter, wanting to blast off so bad, but something held me back. "You know I'm speaking the truth. Whoever took out Supreme had their own agenda. It was just easy for the blame to fall on me because of what went down between us."

"Well, if it wasn't you then who?" I was more confused then ever. I was dead set on believing Nico was the culprit, but my gut knew he was telling the truth. It wasn't him.

"Honestly, I don't know, but it wasn't me; that I can promise you." I was so caught up in digesting what Nico was saying I never heard the front door opening. Before I knew it I had a gun pointing at me and now my life was flashing before my eyes.

"Bitch, put that gun down before I waste you." I turned to see who had me jammed up, and I couldn't believe my eyes.

"Yo, I know you ain't part of this bullshit!" I said shaking my head.

"The two of you know each other?" Nico asked with bewilderment on his face.

"Yeah, I know Precious very well. I was gonna surprise you, baby, and deliver this bitch to you, but my girl Talesha told me you never showed for the drop and pick up. I guess she was misinformed."

"Talesha," I repeated out loud. "Oh shit, LeeLee is short for Talesha, ain't this some bullshit. I knew you were a scandalous trick the first time I met you, but I let my guard down and now this." I switched my attention back to Nico. "I can't believe you got this ho on your team. And, Nina, aren't you supposed to be getting married today?"

"What the fuck is going on?" Nico seethed through clenched teeth.

"Precious, put that fuckin' gun down now and kick it toward me," Nina demanded, ignoring Nico. I did as she said, and as I patted the back of my pants ready to grab my other gun, I realized it wasn't there. I quickly remembered that I left it on the backseat of the Range after I knocked out Vita. I was fucked up in the game right now and didn't know how I would get out this shit. I still had my knife, but I didn't believe Nina would let me get close enough to slit her throat.

"Nina, answer my fuckin' question. How you and Precious know each other, and what's this about you getting married?"

"Oh, so you don't know about her fiancé, Jamal?" I decided to run my mouth for as long as possible to buy some time until I figured a way out this bullshit. "Yeah, I was supposed to be a bridesmaid and everything for this trick. So when did you decide you weren't showing up for the wedding, Nina, before or after you planned on killing me?" Nico and I both stared at Nina waiting for a response.

"If you really want to know how this shit popped off I'll break it down for you starting from the beginning," Nina began taking me down memory lane after picking up my gun. "I was the one Nico called when he tried and failed to put you six feet under and had to go on the run. I'm sure he never got around to telling you this, but we used to fuck around until he got caught up in yo' silly ass. So when he needed me I was there so I could prove to him I was a better bitch than you from day one and he made a mistake choosing you over me. The night you came over to Jamal's house for dinner I immediately recognized your face from a picture that Nico still carries around of you. I wanted to kill your ass right there on the spot but instead I decided I would befriend you, and when the time was right, I'd finish the job that Nico couldn't."

"But, Nina, I told you I had put that shit wit' Precious behind me and was moving on."

"Oh, please, and let this bitch get away with ruining your life? She the reason that we broke up in the first place; she's why you went to jail and you on the run. You might've decided to let her get away with it but not me. I had it all worked out. You was supposed to bring your slick ass over here where I was gonna be waiting to empty my gun on you. Of course you had to throw salt in the game and fuck up my plan, but hell, here you are now, so it all worked out."

"Nah, Nina, you ain't takin' her out. Get that shit out yo' head."

"After everything Precious has done you're still choosing her over me? You're still in love with this poisonous bitch?

I'm the one who's been holding it down for you while she running around like she the queen bee. How can you defend her? I got a good man waiting at the altar for me because I want to be with you."

"Yo, don't put that shit on me. I didn't even know you was engaged. You the one that said you wanted to break out of New York wit' me. I told you to stay here and not put your life on hold to be on the run wit' me."

"You left Jamal standing at the altar so you could run away with Nico? And it was you I saw that night I was coming out that restaurant with Mike? That's why this area looks so familiar. I thought my eyes were playing tricks on me because I was tipsy, but you were sneaking in going to see your other man. It was never about Jamal. Couldn't you have broken things off wit' him instead of wasting everybody's time and his money on a damn wedding that you knew would neva happen?"

"Precious, shut the fuck up. This ain't none of your business. You're the cause of all this bullshit anyway. Nico and I would be married with children right now if he had never met you."

"Hold up, Nina. Now you jumping into some other shit. I appreciate all you've done for me, but you can't blame Precious because she had my heart and you didn't. Even if I hadn't met Precious, I still didn't want to wife you. You were always cool people, and that's why when I was jammed up I reached out to you. Sorry shorty, my feelings never ran deeper than that."

Nina looked crushed. If I had my piece right then it would've been the perfect opportunity to take advantage of her vulnerability. But I had nothing to surprise attack her with.

"Fuck that, Precious is a dead bitch," Nina said coldly.

Nico walked forward. "If you shoot Precious, you have to kill me first," he stated, standing in front of me as a shield. I couldn't believe how this episode was playing out. It touched my heart how Nico was putting his life on the line for me, but I didn't think he realized just how far gone Nina was. She would fuck around and kill both of us on some "fuck the world" type shit. That hero shit had no place with Nina. She had a hard-on for me, and her mind was already made up that today I was going to die.

My mind was spinning, determined to find a way out of the mess, when I heard the three shots ringing in the air. I closed my eyes waiting for the sheer force of the bullets to rip through my soul. I figured the first two shots would take Nico down and the third would be for me. After five more seconds I still didn't feel the excruciating pain of a bullet penetrating my skin, so I opened my eyes to see what the hold up was. To my dismay and relief Nina was dead, lying in a puddle of her blood, and Maya had pulled the trigger.

Innocence Lost

"She's dead," were the words that rang out of Nico's mouth when he couldn't find a pulse on Nina. There were no words to describe my shock at seeing Maya holding the gun that killed Nina. But I couldn't let that put me at a standstill.

"Yo, we got to get the fuck outta here. I know somebody heard those gun shots and called the police." First thing I did was pick up the gun Nina took from me. There was no need to wipe anything 'cause I was a pro at this by now. I then grabbed the gun Maya was holding and realized it was the other nine I had left in the car. Maya stood there still staring down at a dead Nina, not believing she was now a murderer. Nico had disappeared to the bedroom, and I assumed he was trying to gather as much of his belongings as possible.

When he came out he was holding a few suitcases. "You couldn't have packed that fast?" I asked.

"I was already packed. I just had to get my luggage from the bedroom closet." I quickly remembered Nina mentioning that the reason she'd left Jamal at the altar was so she could run away with Nico.

"Oh yeah, that's right, well come on you can ride with us."

"I can't, Precious," Nico said solemnly.

"What do you mean you can't?"

"There's too much heat on me right now. You need to go. I'll be in touch."

"You promise?"

"Yes, I promise."

"But where will you go? Do you need money?"

"Precious, I'll be fine. You know how I get down. You just take care of yourself and be careful. Supreme's killer is still out there."

"I'm sorry, Nico, I'm sorry for everything." Nico put his finger over my lips and kissed me on my forehead before swiftly moving out the front door. I did a quick glance around the apartment before following his lead. On my way out I made one last stop at Nina's dead body. I lifted Nina's finger and slid off the engagement ring Jamal gave her. Now that bitch was free to burn in hell.

I clutched Maya's hand and we jetted out. Right when I was driving off, two police cars pulled up in front of the building. I was relieved we made it out of there, and my mind drifted to Nico. He didn't deserve living a life on the run. Yeah, it was fucked up that he tried to kill me, but if you followed the code of the streets then I really left him no choice. That was the past. I was free, and he deserved to be, too. Now I had another reason besides revenge to find Supreme's killer, and it was to clear Nico's name. I could always switch up my story about who shot me. Dwelling on guns and murder, I changed gears and shifted to Maya.

"Maya, thank you for saving my life."

"You welcome," she said meekly. I couldn't believe the young girl sitting next to me speaking in a low voice was the same person that committed murder less than fifteen minutes ago.

"Do you want to talk about what happened?" I didn't want

to push Maya, but I thought it was important to give her the opportunity to speak on what went down especially since she wouldn't be able to confide in nobody else.

"I didn't plan on killing her, but I had no choice," Maya stated matter-of-factly.

"How did you know I needed you?"

"I was sitting here waiting for you to come out and about thirty minutes after you went in I peeped the chick who was supposed to be getting married today run into the same building."

"I didn't know you had seen Nina before."

"Remember, I was with you when you went to get fitted for the bridesmaid dress. She was wearing that busted-ass wedding dress."

"That's right," I said, recalling their encounter.

"The first question that popped in my head when I saw her was why she wasn't at her wedding. Then I thought maybe she was coming to get you 'cause you were one of her bridesmaids, but that shit didn't sit right wit' me. I might be young, but I'm no dummy. Mike always told me to follow my instincts and ask questions later."

"Good ol' Mike. So that made you come upstairs with a gun?" At that moment I saw the reflection of myself in Maya. I was angry at myself for allowing her to get all caught up in bullshit that had nothing to do with her. But she had been a blessing in disguise because the little bad-ass bitch had saved my life, and for that I would be eternally grateful.

"No, although I had a funny feeling, my mind wasn't thinking you were in no danger."

"What happened that made you realize I was?"

"Besides you taking forever to come back, I heard noises coming from the trunk of the car," *Oh shit, I forgot all about Vita's ass being stashed in the trunk*, I thought to myself. "At first I thought I was hearing things, but the noise persisted. I checked it out and was too through when I saw a girl tied and gagged stuffed in the back."

"Damn, you didn't let her out, did you?"

"Hell no! Obviously if you had her like that it was for a very good reason. I told the bitch she better shut the fuck up before I dumped her ass in the Hudson River." We both burst out laughing. "But on the real, seeing that girl made my brain start thinking all sorts of crazy shit. As I was climbing back to the front, I peeped your gun sitting on the back seat. I figured you needed your weapon and without it you would be in trouble."

"You got that shit right."

"Mike had taught me how to handle a gun, but never did I think I would be using what I learned today. All I wanted to do was make sure you was okay and give you your gun. But when I got to the door I could hear voices and nobody sounded happy. When I heard the guy say something about Nina would have to kill him in order to get to you, I knew it was time to step up."

"I can't believe you held it down for me like that," I said, staring at Maya for a minute while stopped at a red light.

"Precious, I admired you before I even met you. At first it was because you had been married to this megastar rapper and you looked so pretty in pictures I had seen you in. You seemed to be that bitch. Then when I met you and started spending time with you, I checked how thorough you are. You so smart and 'bout real talk. That day you lectured me about throwing my life away chasing after hustling niggas was such a wake-up call, and I appreciated it. There was no way I was going to let some crazy chick take my newfound mentor away from me."

"So I'm your mentor now? I've been called many things but never that."

"Yeah you are. When I grow up I want to be just like you," Maya said proudly. I reflected on all the things I ever wanted to be in life and mentor was nowhere on the list, but the choice was no longer mine. Maya lost whatever innocence she had left when she killed Nina. Yeah, she was protecting me, but most people don't have it in them to have another human being's blood on their hands. But those who could travel to such dark places had the potential to be a cold-blooded killer if left on that path. I was one of those people, and by the look in Maya's eyes, so was she. I didn't know if I should shed a tear for the hard life she would undoubtedly face or raise my fist for her being a soldier who would never have to take anyone's orders, except for mine.

"Maya, I'm flattered that you look up to me, but to walk in my shoes is not an easy path to follow. We can't change what happened today, but it doesn't mean you have to continue to live your life that way. How I roll, I'm constantly getting down for my crown. That mentality isn't for the soft at heart. You feel me?"

"No doubt, and I don't want it no other way. I want to learn from you, Precious. Give me the bitter and the sweet so I can be that bitch that nobody can fuck over."

"Well, the first thing you have to be clear on is not to speak on anything that happened today. I mean nothing, not even to your brother. This remains between us. You don't reply to any questions unless I already green lighted the answer. There's certain shit that you take to your grave with you and killing Nina is one of them."

"I got you. That's our secret, and Nico's of course."

"Yeah, but don't worry about Nico. He wrote the street handbook, and talking about dirt you do in the streets is off-limits."

"Speaking of Nico, that dude is a cutie. He seem like he in love wit' you."

"He used to be my man before I got with Supreme."

"Oh snap, is that the nigga who shot you?"

"Yep, but that's another Brooklyn tale. I'll give you the spiel on that another time. First, I need to come up with my story for Jamal."

"And don't forget about homegirl in the back. What are you going to do with her?" Once again I almost forgot about Vita's ass. There was no doubt she had to be dealt with.

"You feel like taking a ride?"

"Ma, I'm down for whatever. I got you. I hope I proved that today."

"No doubt."

I headed out the city and got on the turnpike going south. By the time we reached the Jersey shore, the sun had gone down and the sky was lit from a full moon and stars. I parked my car near the edge of the cliff overlooking the shore in a deserted area. I had Maya stay in the front seat as I grabbed the gun she used to kill Nina and went to open the trunk. I knew she was a soldier in training, but I didn't want her to witness me ending Vita's life. It's one thing to kill somebody from behind, but it was something totally different to face death head-on and stare in the eyes of your victim before ending her life. Maya wasn't at that place yet, and part of me hoped she never would be. But if I remained her mentor then it was only a matter of time before she was able to drop bodies like a bad habit.

When I lifted the blanket from Vita's head, she squinted her eyes trying to adjust to the light coming from the sky. She had been in the dark for most of the day, and she no doubt started feeling relief thinking she would finally be free. Then her eyes zeroed in on my gun. The tears began gushing down, and my heart did go out to her. If there was a way I could spare Vita's life I would have, but there wasn't. She was a weak link to everything that went down today. No matter how many times she promised never to speak a word of what she knew, I couldn't take the chance of putting my life in her hands.

I grabbed one of the pillows I kept in the trunk from behind Vita. I took off the pillowcase and put it over her face.

I lifted her head and put the pillow under her and grabbed the other one, using it as a silencer. Vita continued to jerk her body furiously, determined not to die. But after two shots to the head all motion instantly stopped. I then asked Maya to help me as we lifted her body out the trunk and tossed her off the cliff. The shit had to be done. There was just no way around it.

As I drove home, I made one more stop right after we got over the George Washington Bridge and tossed the gun that was used for Nina and Vita's murder in the Hudson River. I then listened to the dozens of messages Jamal left me. I still wasn't ready to speak to him. He obviously hadn't yet heard of Nina's death because his last message sounded more like a jilted lover than one in mourning. After a good night's sleep I planned on speaking to him in the morning and hoped I could get Jamal through what would no doubt be a difficult time.

Early the next morning I was awakened by loud voices. I was fighting to stay in my deep sleep, but the noise was persistent. I had no choice but to get out of bed and see what the commotion was about. When I came out my bedroom it was clear there were male voices having a confrontation. I recognized Nathan's voice and shortly after realized the second was Jamal's.

"Nathan, what's going on?" I yelled from the top of the stairs.

"Move out my way, I need to speak to Precious." Within seconds Jamal appeared as he rushed past Nathan.

"Jamal, what's wrong?"

"Precious, I tried to tell this man you were asleep and to come back later, but he wouldn't budge. Do you want me to throw him out?" Nathan said, foaming at the mouth.

"Nathan, it's okay. You know Jamal is a good friend of mine."

"Yeah, but he needs to respect people's privacy. It's seven in the morning, what type of nonsense is that?"

"Why don't you worry about your job and not the time?" Jamal countered.

"My man, this is part of my job. Precious wasn't expecting you. You should've kept it moving until a decent hour. Now you in here disrupting someone else's household."

"Enough. Nathan, thank you, but you can go. I need to speak with Jamal." Both men frowned at one another as Nathan walked away. Jamal caught me off-guard showing up so early, but I had to focus so he wouldn't get suspicious. Then I noticed Jamal looking up toward the wraparound banister, and I turned to follow the direction of his eyes. Maya had also been awakened by the raucous.

"Who was down here screaming?" she asked, still not fully awake.

"It was a misunderstanding. Go back to sleep." Maya, now more alert, saw Jamal and then glanced at me. She paused for another few seconds and then went back to her room.

"Busy morning," I said casually, trying to alleviate the tension in the air.

"What happened yesterday? Why didn't you show up for the wedding or return my calls?" Jamal's voice was full of accusatory undertones. I knew I had to choose my words wisely.

"Jamal, I'm so sorry. I didn't even have a chance to check my messages. I got so sidetracked with Maya and her problems that I couldn't focus on anything else. But why are you here? Shouldn't you be with your new wife?"

"What problems did Maya have?"

"An abusive boyfriend. Mike is out of town, so I had to take the place of big brother." There was no question in my mind Jamal was now drilling me, and I didn't like it one bit but I remained cool. "So how was the wedding? I know Nina looked absolutely stunning. Her custom made Vera Wang gown was beautiful."

"Yeah, it's too bad I never got to see it on her," Jamal said as he walked up the stairs. The closer he got to me I could see his eyes were swollen and red like he'd been crying all night.

"I don't understand, what happened?"

"Nina never made it to the wedding. In fact, Nina is dead."

"What?!" I belted. I even put my hand over my mouth for extra dramatics. "What happened? Did she get in a car accident or something?"

"No, she was murdered."

"Murdered, but who'd want to kill Nina?" Jamal's eyes stayed locked on mine and I knew he was searching for any sign that I was lying or knew more than what I was saying. I refused to draw back.

"But it gets better. She was involved with Nico Carter."

"Nico Carter," I repeated, sounding confused.

"Yes, your ex and the man who tried to murder you."

"I know who Nico Carter is, but I had no idea he knew Nina. How did you find that out?"

"Shortly after they discovered Nina's body they checked her last outgoing and incoming calls which led them to Talesha. After hearing about Nina's death she broke down and told the cops everything. Including Nina's relationship with Nico and helping orchestrate a set up involving you."

"Nina and Talesha—that same loud-mouth chicken that was up in my face at the bridal gown boutique? I was hanging with the enemies and didn't even know it. I can't believe they were trying to set me up, but for what?"

"Supposedly she resented your past relationship with Nico and held you responsible for him being on the run."

"This all sounds crazy and far-fetched." While continuing my act of being dumbfounded I secretly wished I had tossed Talesha over the cliff along with Vita. But luckily I did have Vita tell her I was a no show. Still, Talesha was so besieged by the death of Nina she'd developed diarrhea of the mouth. To kill her now would put unwanted heat on me, so hopefully the police and Jamal would chalk up both women as being the scandalous, grimy whores they are, or in Nina's case, were.

"At first I did, too, but after the cops told me they found Nico's fingerprints throughout her apartment, and a lady that runs the building identified him in a picture. That combined with Talesha's story made me realize it had to be true. But once I thought about it, it all made sense. I suspected Nina was seeing somebody, but I could never prove it. Then when you didn't come up with any dirt I wanted to believe my suspicions were incorrect."

"So have the police located Nico, and do they think he's responsible for Nina's death?"

"No, once again the elusive Nico has managed to disappear, but the police aren't really saying if they believe he is the shooter. One of the detectives did tell me they believe whoever killed her snuck up from behind. This entire ordeal is extraordinary because never did I see all these lies coming. Nina was living a whole other life that I was completely unaware of. It's funny how you think you know someone so well, but come to find out you don't know them at all. They're a complete stranger."

"I know what you mean." I wasn't quite sure if Jamal's comment was directed at his life with Nina or me, but it was time for him to go. "Jamal, I don't mean to rush you out, but I need to take care of some things. But let's definitely talk later on." I gave Jamal a hug and started walking back up the stairs.

"Aren't you curious to know what Nina's intentions were when she tried to set you up?" Jamal blurted out, freezing my step.

"Why don't you tell me?"

"Your death."

"It seems a lot of people want me dead."

"Indeed, but you always seem to be one step ahead."

"Is there something you want to ask me, Jamal? Because if so then just do it." It was clear from my tone that my patience with Jamal had run out.

"Did you kill Nina?" he asked point blank.

"As a matter of fact I didn't. And I resent you even making the implication."

"I have the right to know what happened to my fiancée," he said, becoming defensive.

"The so called fiancée, who not only left you at the altar but was carrying on a full-fledged relationship with a known cold-blooded killer, is that the fiancée you're harassing me about? Let me give you a little bit of advice. Stop wasting your time playing Perry Mason for a woman who obviously didn't give a damn about you."

"That's cold."

"What's cold is you cross-examining me this early in the morning in my own home. I'm beginning to regret not letting Nathan show you the front door. But I'll give you a pass this one time because Nina's death has apparently left you delusional. That can be the only explanation for your blatant disrespect. Now please leave my home before I have to call security."

"Precious, wait. I'm sorry. You not showing up at the wedding and then not returning my phone calls, then the Nico factor has my mind working overtime. This whole bizarre episode has me feeling like I'm in the twilight zone. I'm taking my frustrations out on you, and I apologize."

"Like I said I'm giving you a pass this one time, but I think it is best you leave—you've already said enough." I continued walking up the stairs, dismissing his presence. Jamal needed to be well aware of my anger so he would think twice before discussing his suspicions of me with anybody else. I didn't hold too many people in a high esteem, but Jamal was one of them. I would hate to take him out this world because of his misplaced love for a ruthless bitch. I hoped for Jamal's sake he would let sleeping dogs lie.

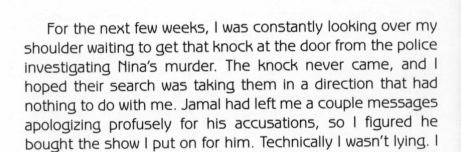

It's Personal

For the next few weeks, I was constantly looking over my shoulder waiting to get that knock at the door from the police investigating Nina's murder. The knock never came, and I hoped their search was taking them in a direction that had nothing to do with me. Jamal had left me a couple messages apologizing profusely for his accusations, so I figured he bought the show I put on for him. Technically I wasn't lying. I didn't kill Nina, but it was only because I wasn't given the chance. It would've been my pleasure to lullabye her sneaky ass.

Before I could delve any deeper, my thoughts were interrupted by the ringing of my cell phone.

"Hello."

"Precious, please come and get me," a frantic Maya screamed.

"What's wrong, and where are you?"

"I'm in the Bronx. I got into a fight with my boyfriend, and he straight left me stranded here with no cash, no cell, nothing. I'm using some dude's phone that I don't even know."

"Relax. Give me your exact location and I'll come get you." I typed the address in my navigation system and made a detour from going to get my nails done so I could scoop up Maya. I hadn't seen her since her suspension was up and she went back to school. I figured everything was going cool, but it was the middle of the week during school hours and instead of being in class, Miss Fast-Ass Maya was standing on some corner in the Bronx.

I slowed down when I got on Baychester Avenue and looked for Maya. I noticed her standing on the corner by the Barnes and Noble. I beeped my horn and she came running up to the car with a smile across her face. Besides her hair being a little disheveled I didn't see any noticeable bruises which was a relief.

"Precious, you're the best. I was out here 'bout to freak out," Maya said, getting in the car.

"What the hell happened, and who is this boyfriend you got? I hope it ain't that older dude you mentioned before."

"Nah, I don't deal wit' him no more. Clip's dumb ass did this shit to me."

"Clip? How old is he, and how long you been dealing wit' dude? And why he leave you stranded in the Bronx?" I had to stop myself because the questions kept rolling off my tongue.

"He just turned eighteen. We been kicking it for a couple of months now, but keeping it on the hush hush 'cause he work for my brother. That's what we got in the fight about. I want us to step out as a couple and come clean but he talking 'bout no."

"What he do for your brother?"

"He push weight." Maya gave me a screw face as if I should've known that.

"Your brother still moving diesel out here? I thought he gave all that up for this music game."

"Getting that music shit to keep poppin' off cost a lot

more paper than Mike anticipated, so he use the drug game to fund the music game. Plus, you know my brother gon' be street for life." I nodded my head listening to Maya, becoming increasingly curious about what she was spitting to me.

"But see Clip, he tryna break into the business as a rapper. My brother was supposed to sign him to his label, and today he told me it's about to happen, and that's why he ain't ready to let everybody know we together. I'm like, shit, fuck dat, what you care more about my brother putting you on than being wit' me?"

"What changed to make Mike want to sign him to his label now?" Maya was halfway listening to me and partly listening to the radio. When Ludacris' *"Money Maker"* came on she turned up the volume and snapped her fingers.

"That's my song right there. But yeah, um, what changed was Supreme getting murdered." I hit the brakes so suddenly on my Range that if the car behind me had been just a few feet closer it would've rammed right into me. The person in the back of me started blowing the horn, but now the light was red so everybody was on pause. I cut the radio off with quickness and turned to Maya. "Why you turn that off? I told you that's my song," Maya complained.

"Maya, what did Supreme's death have to do with that nigga Clip?"

"Well you know Supreme had the rap shit on lock. He was King of New York. Couldn't nobody new come out and really get no shine. My brother was actually tryna get Supreme to sign to his label."

"You must've got your information wrong."

"No, I don't. I was there, I heard the conversation," Maya said twisting her neck.

"What conversation?" Now every car behind me was blowing their horn because the light had turned green, but I was so entranced by what Maya was saying I hadn't noticed. After going through the light, I pulled over on the side of the street. I didn't want no further interruptions.

"Over the summer I was staying wit' Mike, and he gave me some money to go shopping 'cause like always he had some business to handle and wanted me gone. I didn't care, but when I was about to leave I overheard him saying Supreme would be there in a few. Girl, you know I lost it. I wasn't positive it was 'the' Supreme," Maya said giving the quotation sign with her hands, "but the chance that it was was worth me sticking around for.

"Mike always had his meetings in his entertainment room, so when he stepped out I hid in one of the closets and waited, determined to see my boo. Precious, I hope you don't feel I'm being disrespectful. I know he was your husband, but I'd been in love wit' him since he did that record with Beyonce, '*Wife You*.' Me and my girls just knew he was talking about us." Maya was grinning telling me her story and not understanding I could give a flying fuck about the crush she and every other chick on these streets had on Supreme. My interest was on Mike.

"It's cool, finish your story."

"Yeah, yeah, so finally Supreme did show up looking fine. He had on the white Sean John sweat suit, all iced out. The damn rock he had in his ear was blinding me from the closet."

"Enough about what he was wearing, tell me about the conversation."

"It wasn't nothin' too deep. Mike basically told Supreme that he knew his deal was up with whatever label he was on, and he wanted Supreme to sign wit' him. Mike threw out all these huge dollar amounts he'd give him. See that's how I know my brother so paid. That's why I don't have no problem hittin' him up all the time for paper and dare him to say no 'cause I know all that money he was offering Supreme. You feel me?" I just nodded my head so Maya could continue spilling the information.

"Uh huh, so yeah, Mike was tryna offer Supreme more money than what Bill Gates got, and when they finished talking both of them left. And thank goodness they did 'cause I was loving seeing my boo, Supreme, but I had to pee."

"You haven't told me what Supreme said to Mike's offer."

"Oh, Supreme told Mike hell-to-the-no. So I knew Supreme had extra long paper too, to turn all that money down."

"When did all this go down?" I could see Maya straining her brain trying to remember.

"Come to think of it, it was a week before Supreme got killed. I remembered I was listening to Miss Jones on Hot 97 and she made the announcement, and I was like damn, I just saw him last week. But least I was lucky enough to see Supreme in the flesh, none of my girls can say that. But real talk, I cried when I heard Supreme was dead. Are the police any closer to finding his killer?"

"Nope." *But I am*, I thought to myself. I didn't say a word as I drove Maya back to my house. She was so busy singing and rapping to every song on the radio that she was oblivious to the dark places my mind had gone after our conversation. I was always so positive Nico was the triggerman in Supreme's death that I never let my mind go in another direction. Had the detectives who came to see me right after Supreme's murder been right? Was Supreme always the intended mark? Was this about music and money, not revenge? I had to find out once and for all.

When we pulled up to the crib, Maya snapped out of her musical bliss and focused her attention back on me.

"Precious, you're not going tell my brother about what went down today, are you?"

"You mean in regards to Clip?"

"Yeah, what else would I be talking 'bout?" Maya asked, not having a clue how valuable the conversation that she overheard between her brother and Supreme was to me.

"Nah, I wasn't asking, I was making a statement. Don't worry, I won't mention a word to Mike about Clip. But you do need to be careful. That nigga left you in the Bronx wit' no money, no purse, nothing. Do you really want a cat like that as your man?"

"I forgot to mention that I did use my purse and phone to go upside his head when he told me we still couldn't tell nobody about our relationship."

"But you said y'all got into a fight."

"Yeah, we fought wit' our mouths, and then I fought him wit' my fist, purse and phone."

"So what did he do?"

"Latched onto my arms all tight, then took my phone and purse before driving off." Maya smacked her lips and folded her arms like she was the victim.

"So he didn't hit you?"

"Hell nah. Clip ain't crazy. He know I'd tell my brother and that nigga be dead. But he need to give me my shit back. The only reason I didn't call Mike was 'cause I didn't want him knowing I skipped school."

"I tell you what. Everything we talked about will stay between us. There's no need for Mike to know you skipped school. But chill on the Clip situation, he'll give you back your stuff."

"So you think he's right for wanting to keep our relationship a secret?"

"It's not about right and wrong, it's about getting what you want. You have to know which battles to fight and which aren't worth stressing over. If you're meant to be with Clip, then it'll happen. Relax, ma."

"A'ight, I'll follow your advice. But how we gon' explain to Mike why I'm at your crib?"

"I'll handle Mike. I'll tell him I'ma pick you up from school so we can have a girls' day. You can spend the night, and I'll drop you to school in the morning."

"That's what's up! You're the best, Precious."

"Hum huh, but you will be going to school tomorrow. Don't fuck around with your education, Maya. It's vital to have that street knowledge but just as important to hit them books. I still regret not going to college and maybe one day I will, but having your high school diploma is a must," I said, dead serious.

"Damn, I never really thought that deeply about it before but you right. I promise I'll get my act together and start hittin' them books."

"I'm proud of you, now get out the car. I got moves to make. Nathan will let you in."

"But wait, I thought you said we were having a girls' day?" Maya said with a frown on her face.

"That's what I'm telling your brother. I have some things that need to be handled, but when I get back we can hit the mall and go out to eat or something." Maya's fact lit back up at my offer. "Okay, I'll see you when I get back."

I waited and made sure Maya got in the house before driving off. I did have moves to make. First thing I did was place a call to Jamal. I hadn't spoken to him since he tried to go Perry Mason on my ass, but from the messages he left me it seemed he let it go, though the reception I received on the phone would be the only way I'd know for sure.

"Hello," Jamal answered.

"Hi, Jamal, it's me, Precious."

"Wow, I can't believe it's you. I'm surprised to hear your voice."

"My number didn't come up on your phone?"

"Honestly, I was in the middle of something and didn't even check it before I picked up. But I'm really happy to hear from you. After our last conversation I didn't think I would ever speak to you again. I was completely out of line." I was relieved to know Jamal had fallen for my performance because I needed his help.

"You were in shock. You'd just found out Nina was dead. I understand you were looking for someone to blame."

"You're a bigger person than me, Precious. I appreciate your forgiveness. So how's everything with you?"

"It's coming along. But it could be better if you could do me favor."

"Whatever you need."

"Thanks, but I'd rather not discuss it over the phone. Can I meet you at your office later on today?"

"Sure, what time?"

"Around four."

"That works for me."

"Great, I'll see you then." After hanging up with Jamal I placed my next phone call, which was to Mike. After the fourth ring I thought my call would go to voicemail but then he picked up.

"What did I do to deserve a call from you?" The suaveness in Mike's voice almost made me forget what I was scheming on.

"You're so silly. I wanted to let you know that I'ma pick Maya up from school and let her spend the night with me. I haven't seen her since she went back to school, and I thought we could have a big sister, little sister day."

"Maya would like that. She looks up to you. Personally, I think the two of you are a lot alike."

"Yeah, she's a little mini-me. I'm definitely gonna look out for her."

"How 'bout me? It seemed at one time I was making progress and we had a shot at being together, but then you just backed away. What's up with that?"

"I was going through a lot with Supreme's death then that shit with Jalen. I took that as a sign that I wasn't ready to jump into anything serious."

"I feel you, but what about now?"

"That's the other reason I called. I wanted to see if we could pick up where we left off, unless you've moved on."

"No, I'm still here. I was waiting for you to get it together and realize I'm the only nigga for you."

"Then how 'bout tomorrow? We can start off by going out for dinner."

"I have a better idea. How about I cook you dinner?"

"You can cook?"

"Can I? If I wasn't in the music game I would've opened up a chain of restaurants and been my own chef."

"Big talk, I hope you can deliver."

"Trust, you'll be impressed."

"Then it's a date. I'll see you tomorrow night around seven?"

"That works. You and Maya have fun."

"We will, bye." I couldn't lie to myself. I wanted to be wrong about my suspicions regarding Mike. From the first time I laid eyes on him at the club I felt some sort of attraction. It wasn't just his jaw-dropping looks, he had an authoritative presence. No matter how expensive the suit or charming the smile there was no escaping that he was a straight up thug which is the only type of man I crave.

If I was wrong about Mike then the possibilities were endless. If I was right, and he was responsible for ripping Supreme out my life, then he would no doubt have to pay with his life. For my sake and Maya's I prayed that I was wrong. I was rattled out of my thoughts by the ring of my cell. The call was from a blocked number. "Hello."

"Is anyone around you?"

"Nico, is that you?'

"Judging by the fact that you shouted out my name, I take it that you're alone?" I let out a slight chuckle at the sarcasm in his voice.

"Sorry 'bout that, but I was so surprised to hear your voice. But yeah, I'm alone. How are you?"

"Just keepin' low."

"Are you still in the area?"

"Yeah, I'm tryna tie up some loose ends before I head out of here. If you don't mind I would like to see you before I leave."

"I wanna see you, too. When are you leaving?"

"Tomorrow morning. You think we can meet tonight?"

"Tonight is good." I promised Maya we would hang out, but I really needed to see Nico for my own reasons. I would make it up to her.

"Cool, I'll call you around eight to let you know where to come. Make sure you're careful. I can't afford you being tracked by anybody."

"I got you. I'll be waiting for your call." When I got off the phone with Nico I called Maya. She was disappointed that I had to cancel, but I bribed her by saying I would take her shopping at Short Hills Mall. That ended all the huffing and puffing. I then finished running my errands so I wouldn't be late for my meeting with Jamal.

When I arrived at Jamal's office, he was finishing up a staff meeting. It was still somewhat hard to believe that the same nerdy boy with glasses who popped my cherry was now running Atomic Records, one of the biggest urban labels in the world.

"Precious, come in. It's so nice to see you." Jamal gave me a hug and an innocent kiss on the cheek. When he closed his office door he once again started with the apologies. "I'm sorry about what happened. I feel awful for accusing you of killing Nina. To even think you are capable of murder is idiotic in itself. Please forgive me."

"Jamal, you've said sorry more than enough, and I accept your apology. So please stop, it isn't necessary. I know how hard it is to lose a loved one. Are the police any closer to finding Nina's killer?"

"Not yet," Jamal said as he sat down in his plush leather chair that had an unbelievable view of New York City as its backdrop. Of course they're still trying to track down Nico."

"What about the girl you said they were questioning?"

"Oh, yes, Talesha. She hasn't been able to assist the police any further. She never even met Nico. Some other woman that was working with them was also found dead by the Jersey Shore."

"Do the police believe the cases are related?"

"They've been digging deeply into their lives and each of the women was shady including Nina. Most of the scams they pulled were on a low level, but maybe they crossed the wrong person. Who knows, but it's hard to believe that I was in love with and about to marry such a deceitful woman. Do you know that Nina also used to be a drug carrier? That's how she started dealing with Nico."

"What? So when did she stop?"

"Honestly, I don't know if she did stop. Although I took care of Nina, she always had her own money. One of the reasons I was impressed with her was because she seemed independent. When I would ask her how she kept so much cash, she'd say it was from her modeling gigs. I was stupid to believe that, especially since I never saw her in anything but a few music videos, and we all know how much those pay. One can truly be blinded by love, that's for sure."

I was absorbing the crazy life of Nina. Her whole groupie girl persona was an act. She was a straight street bitch, that's why she had no problem pulling her gun out on me ready to kill. But what was the act for? To get to Jamal or me? The more I found out the more confused I became.

"Enough about Nina. What can I do for you? You said something about a favor on the phone."

"Yes. This is extremely important, Jamal. I need this done right away and with discretion."

"Spill."

"I need for you to draw up a contract from Atomic Records to buy the rights to Supreme's masters. I need for it to look authentic with real dollar amounts that even the most music savvy business person would believe. I need them by tomorrow morning." Jamal swallowed hard and I could tell by his eye movement his mind was spinning.

"What's going on, Precious?" he asked seriously. Jamal then stood up and walked around his desk so he was now standing next to me. Maybe he thought being closer to me would allow him to get a better read as to what was going on in my head.

"Will you do it or not?"

"It's not that simple."

"Yes, it is."

"Are you saying that the contract I'll have our lawyers draft up, you'll sign?"

"I'm saying I need the contract and what I do with it afterwards is still up in the air."

"That means 'no.' So, who are you trying to convince that this contract is real and why?"

"Jamal, the less you know the better."

"If you want me to help you, then I need answers, real answers." I debated in my mind for a second whether I wanted to go there with Jamal. I desperately needed that contract because without it my plan would never have the same effect.

"I believe I know who had something to do with Supreme's murder, and that contract will give me the ammunition I need to provoke them."

"But you made it clear that you believe Nico killed Supreme. Nico didn't have anything to do with the music business, so what is the contract for?"

"Nico didn't kill Supreme."

"How would you know that?"

"I just do. So please don't ask me any more questions.

Are you going to help me or not?" I could tell by the intense stare that Jamal was giving me he had a strong suspicion that I had seen Nico. I knew that would lead to more questions surrounding the death of Nina. Jamal wanted answers, but now wasn't the time for me to give them.

"I'll do what you ask, but one day you will sit down and answer all of my questions. You owe me that."

"Thank you. I'll pick up the contracts tomorrow. I really have to go. But thanks again." I rushed out of Jamal's office, not giving him a chance to speak another word. I had nothing more to say to Jamal until I was able to get the closure I was seeking. I needed to be free from all the bullshit from the past and start my life on a clean slate. After tomorrow night I hoped it would be the end of the past and a start to a new beginning.

After leaving Jamal, I picked up a few items from Saks and then headed to the W Hotel in Times Square. I didn't want to drive all the way back to my house in Jersey or answer a bunch of questions from Maya, so checking into a hotel was the most convenient option. I took a long hot shower thinking about what surprises would present themselves in the near future. I wondered if tonight would be the last time I would ever see Nico again and if tomorrow evening I'd be putting a bullet through Mike's heart. What I did know was after closing this chapter in my life, I wanted to fall in love again, settle down and start a family. One that was free of drama and the street life. I no longer wanted the gun to be my best friend. I was a step away from completely losing my soul, and soon it would be too late to save myself.

By the time I finished pulling my hair back in a sleek pony tail and slipping on a metallic colored jumpsuit with a wide black belt that cinched my waist, Nico had called. He gave me an address in Staten Island to meet him. I dabbed on some lip gloss, grabbed my Jimmy Choo Mahala tote bag and headed out the hotel room.

Luckily, I knew my way around Staten Island because the address Nico gave me didn't even come up in my navigation system. The nondescript building was somewhere in the cut on a dead end street. The only reason I was able to find it was because I used to hit up this mom and pop soul food restaurant down the hill every once in awhile.

As directed by Nico, I drove my car down the steep hill driveway and parked in the back. From the short distance I saw someone peep through the blinds and figured it was Nico. When I got to the door it was already ajar. At first I hesitated, but when I heard Nico telling me to come in I felt more comfortable.

"How did you find this place?" was the first question out my mouth.

"I still know a few people who got hideout spots."

"This is definitely one of those, ain't nobody gonna find you here. But the inside of this place is nice," I said, observing the lush carpet, stainless steel kitchen appliances and huge open space. You would never think all this was going on from looking at the outside.

"Yeah, it's pretty official for what it is. But I'm ready to break out."

"Have you decided where you're going?"

"Yep, but don't ask me where. If you ever get yourself jammed up and they question you about my whereabouts, I really want you to be able to say you don't know. It's for your own protection."

"Am I gonna ever see you again?"

"I hope. I'll keep in touch from time to time. But if and when I get word that I'm able to show my face again then you know I'm coming home. New York is truly all I know."

"Nico, you don't have to worry about the charges sticking for shooting me. If they do come at you, I'll tell them I made a mistake and you weren't the person who tried to kill me. I'll get on the stand and testify to that if I have to."

"I don't know what to say. Since I've been on the run all I've done was think. Think about my life, the past and of course, you. It's still hard to believe that this is how everything turned out. When I first got out of jail I was so full of rage and had nothing but contempt toward you. But there is such a thin line between love and hate. And in my heart I never stopped loving you, and even now I wish we could be together and start our life all over again someplace else. But I know that's not possible. I have to clear my name and maybe then if you still feel the same way we can try again."

"I can't lie, my feelings for you do still run deep. Just like I hope you've forgiven me for fucking up your life, I've forgiven you for putting a bullet in my chest. I don't know if we can ever be together again, but I do believe the police will find Supreme's killer, whether the person is dead or alive. Then you will be able to come back and fight the charges they have against you for attempted murder."

"What do you mean find Supreme's killer either dead or alive? Do you know who took him out?"

"Just like you don't want to tell me where you're going, this is something that I need to keep to myself. But if it all works out, after you disappear, the next time you call me I'll have good news."

"I know how you are, Precious, so I'm not going to pressure you. All I will say is be careful. Whoever took out Supreme is ruthless, and they're playing for keeps. I don't want anything to happen to you," Nico said, now standing within kissing distance. He lifted my chin and softly brushed his lips against mine. He paused, waiting for my reaction.

"Don't stop," I whispered. I didn't want Nico to stop. I wanted to feel what it was like for him to be inside of me again. Besides Supreme, he was the only man I ever loved. Being with Nico would numb the pain I had in my heart from losing Supreme if only for one night.

Nico lifted me up and carried me to a bedroom in the back. We both slowly undressed one another, taking in every inch of each other's bodies. The king-sized bed was so inviting. My warm body melted into the silk sheets. Nico's kisses trickled down from my lips to my neck, and when I felt the moistness of his mouth swallow my breast, I let out a yearning moan. Then he stopped. I opened my eyes and saw him staring at me. With his fingers he traced the faint scar down the middle of my chest where the doctors cut me open. I turned away. I couldn't bear to see him see what he did to me. Pushing his hands away, I pulled him closer. "Baby, put it in. I need that dick inside of me, now," I moaned.

"Wait." Nico's fingers drifted down toward my legs where he spread them open and buried his face in my juices. He used his mouth to fuck my pussy, and it was driving me crazy. I sank my nails deep into his smooth, milk chocolate, butter-soft skin. Right when I was about to explode he entered inside of me gratifying my every desire. The way he rocked in my pussy with such ease made me reflect back to when our life together was so fucking lovely. We were the king and queen of the streets. I was ready to ride it out with Nico to the fullest, but shit changed. Making love with him again brought back old feelings, and while being caught up in his rapture, the sorrow engrossing my life vanished. When we both reached the height of pleasure we climaxed simultaneously and fell asleep in each other's arms.

Tossing and turning in sleep, I halfway opened my eyes and saw that is was six o'clock in the morning. Although I wanted to fall back in Nico's arms I remembered I had to take Maya to school in the morning. I quickly threw on my clothes and sat back on the bed staring at a still sleeping Nico. He looked so peaceful lying there. I kissed him on the forehead and softly said, "I love you," hoping this wouldn't be the last time I would be with him.

When I arrived home I only had enough time to take a shower. While I was getting dressed I heard Maya knocking at my door.

"Come in."

"Dang you up all bright and early. What time did you get in last night?"

"About midnight," I answered, straight lying.

"Oh, 'cause I tried to wait up for you but fell asleep around eleven. Where did you go?"

"I stopped through Brooklyn to see some old friends. Ended up staying much longer than I thought I would, so what's up?"

"Yeah, I didn't bring no clothes for school. So since we 'bout the same size I wanted to borrow something cute 'cause you be rockin' nothing but the official gear."

"Well, I have some Juicy Couture sweat suits that you can put on."

"I like Juicy Couture. What color you got?"

"Every color. Go pick out whichever one you want. While

you're getting dressed I'll have Anna make us something to eat."

"Thanks, Precious. I love staying here with you. You're like the big sister I never had."

"You never know, maybe it can become permanent."

"You mean that?"

"No doubt. I like having you around. But get dressed, I don't want you to be late for school." The idea of having Maya live with me was one I looked forward to. It was lonely living in this big-ass house all by myself. It was obvious from little statements Maya would make that the relationship with her mother was strained, and that was putting it lightly. Maya made it clear that she didn't like her mother's boyfriend and even made reference to him crossing the line with her on more than one occasion. I wanted to mention it to Mike, but some men are extra sensitive when it comes to discussing anything negative about their mothers, so I decided to hold off.

Regardless, I could relate to Maya living in a household under miserable conditions. I had that relationship with my mother my whole life—having to deal with watching her sell her body to fund an out-of-control drug addiction. That is the sort of agony no child should have to endure. By the time my mother did finally get her life together, and we had a chance at a real relationship, she, too was ripped out of my life by the greediness of the streets.

"Precious, it's after eight, we need to go," Maya said as I sat in the kitchen zoning out.

"Damn, you scared me. My mind was someplace else. I can't believe you rushing me to get to school."

"I'm looking all cute in my outfit I want to floss. Plus I slept so good last night, I feel rested."

"I bet you do, but remember you gotta focus and hit them books."

"I know, and I will."

"Good, let me get my keys and we're out."

When I pulled up to Maya's school she was eager to get out. "Thanks again, Precious, for the ride, the clothes and letting me spend the night. Don't forget you still owe me a girls' day."

"I haven't. I'll call you later on. Make sure you stay in school all day," I emphasized.

"I will. Just make sure you don't forget about me." I stared at Maya strangely, finding it odd she would even say that.

"How can I forget about you, we're like family now. No matter what goes down, we're like this," I said, crossing my fingers to show that meant we were tight. "Now get in there and kick some ass, not literally, I mean them books." We both laughed and Maya shut the door.

Keeping to my plans for the day, I headed to Midtown to pick up the contract from Jamal. To save me the headache of having to park, Jamal left a message letting me know to call up to his office, and he would have someone bring them down for me. I did just that and within a few minutes I had the envelope in my hand. I opened it and saw that he had given me three copies. I briefly glanced through the paperwork, and without a doubt they looked legit. When I got to the last page of the contract it had the line that required my signature to seal the deal.

Having secured the contract, the most vital part of my plan, I then stopped at a spyware shop and got the final piece for my scheme. I ordered a custom-made wrist watch that could do up to nine hours of voice recording. If Mike did turn out to be Supreme's murderer, after I got him to admit it on tape I would end his life. I would have the tape edited so only Mike's confession would be heard and then send it to the detective overseeing the investigation. I don't like fucking with cops, but I had to do something to guarantee Nico was never charged with Supreme's murder.

Needing to relax my mind and body for my encounter with Mike later on that evening, I spent the rest of the day at the spa getting pampered. I had to relax and mentally prepare myself for what might go down with Mike. He was a highly intelligent and dangerous man. I had to be on top of my game to not set off any red flags.

When I got into the passenger seat of my baby blue Bentley, I was prepared and ready for war. I had my documents neatly folded in my purse. At the right moment all I had to do was discreetly flip a switch, and my wrist watch would begin recording. And of course, I had my bitch with me. When and if it was time, she would be ready to lullabye Mike.

I slowly pulled up to his crib, keeping my nerves intact. Killing wasn't new to me, but for some reason I was a little on edge. I rang the doorbell and within a few seconds Mike opened the door. He was looking extra fine in a pair of russet-colored pants with a cream cashmere v-neck sweater that fit perfectly on his 6'2" frame.

"You look stunning," Mike said, commenting on my winter white ensemble.

"Thanks, I was thinking the same thing about you." I walked inside and was impressed with the layout of Mike's home. "This is nice. I've never been to your house before."

"That's right. It's not as luxurious as the estate you live on, but it's cool for a single bachelor."

"I bet you've had plenty of women trying to turn this bachelor pad into a family home." I couldn't blame them. The décor was off the chain. The house was roughly 3,000 square feet with floors that seemed to be marble throughout. I was tempted to take off my shoes, but since Mike didn't ask I let my heels continue to click across the floor.

"I don't bring women here."

"Last time I checked I'm a woman."

"Let me rephrase that. I don't bring just any woman here, only the special ones."

"How many times have you used that line and does it really work?" I was trying to give Mike a hard time but I believed he was telling the truth. The first rule with any nigga who hustled on the streets was keep where you lay your head a secret, especially from bitches. You never knew if one would flip out on you and set you up so the next man could rob you.

"This is the first, so you tell me, did it work?"

"I guess you'll know by the end of the night. But I do know something smells delicious. What did you cook?"

"See for yourself." Mike led me to the dining room where a beautiful candlelight dinner awaited. The table was positioned in front of a huge glass window with a view of the swimming pool. "I made a few dishes, some tagliolini lobster, ravioli marsala, ossobuco and pappardelle."

"You weren't kidding when you said you can cook. I can't even pronounce some of that stuff. But the food smells off the hook, so let's eat."

For the next hour, Mike and I kicked around conversation about different topics but nothing major, but then Mike turned serious.

"Having you here, sharing this dinner with you makes me realize how much I've been missing. I've spent the last few years working so hard that I had almost forgotten the importance of companionship, especially when it's with someone you're really feeling."

"I know what you mean. Since losing Supreme there has been a void in my life. I wasn't ready to let go—being in so much pain actually gave me a part of him to hold on to. But I know Supreme would want me to be happy and to find love again."

"Could you see yourself being in love with me?"

"Honestly, I could." Mike stood up and walked over to a

small stand and opened the drawer. He pulled out a long silver box and came back over to the table.

"Open it." My eyes widened when I saw the flawless diamond necklace sparkling at me. "Take that necklace off; let me put this on," Mike said, taking the necklace from the box.

"Wait, this is the necklace Supreme gave me, and I never take it off."

"You can take it off this one time. Please wear it tonight, and you can put the one Supreme gave you back on tomorrow."

"Okay." He unclasped Supreme's necklace and handed it to me. I held it tightly in my hand. I was in shock that Mike had given me such a pricey piece of jewelry even though we still weren't a couple.

"It looks beautiful on you."

"It's rare, but I'm at a lost for words. I can't believe you got this for me."

"You're the type of woman I could see myself being with. Giving you this necklace was a small way of showing you that."

"Mike, you're incredible. Not only am I attracted to you physically, but you have great taste in jewelry and I respect your street and business savvy."

"Thank you. I'm actually still deciding which one is more cutthroat. The street game can be brutal, but the music business is just as lethal, if not more. You're dealing with so much money and everybody is trying to get their share of the pot." As I listened to Mike preach about the music industry, I realized that this was the right opportunity to strike. While he continued to talk and poured himself a glass of wine I switched on the button to start recording.

"I'm glad you brought up how vicious the music business can be, because I almost forgot about some papers I wanted you to take a look at for me. I'm taking them to my lawyers in the morning, but it never hurts to have another pair of sharp eyes read over something this important."

"Sure, baby. What you want me to read over?" I unzipped my purse and pulled out the envelope with the neatly folded contract.

"Here, if you don't mind, take a look at this." I handed Mike the contract, and he put his glass down, giving the documents his full attention. I watched as he read intently, flipping each page. His body remained calm but I could see the vein pulsating in his neck revealing his anxiety.

"I know you're not going to sign this," Mike said, tossing the contract on the table.

"Why do you say that? I think $25 million is more than a fair offer. There are also bonus stipulations and other perks, including royalties."

"I thought you said that you would give me an opportunity to make an offer before selling to Atomic."

"I never said that. I had no idea you were even interested, especially since Supreme wasn't one of your favorite people."

"You don't remember me telling you to come to me before you accepted Jamal's or anyone else's offer for Supreme's masters?"

"I recall you mentioning it briefly, but I chose not to take you up on that offer. But I'm letting you look at them now." I smiled, purposely antagonizing Mike, hoping to rile him up.

"Yeah, after the lawyers for Atomic already drew up these bullshit papers. You can't sign this," Mike belted as he picked up the contract and tore it up.

"What are you doing?"

Mike slammed his hand down on the table. "Precious, I'm only protecting you. Jamal isn't offering you enough. You shouldn't even sell Supreme's masters. You should go into business for yourself, and I can be your partner. We can put Supreme's music out on my label, make that *our* label."

"So you're offering me half of your company for what, the

rights to Supreme's music?"

"Yes, we can do this together not only as business part-ners but as husband and wife." Talk about desperation, the nerve of Mike to give me some fake-ass marriage proposal so he could control Supreme's material. I knew once I signed over the rights I would have been signing my death certifi-cate as well.

"Huh, you can't be serious. I don't want to be in the music business, and I'm definitely not ready to jump into a mar-riage with someone I don't know shit about. I mean you have serious control issues, tearing up my contract—that's insane."

"I can't let you sign those papers."

"You think ripping up the contract is going to change my mind? I do have other copies you know."

"Don't do this, Precious," Mike grabbed my arm with a solid hold.

"Let go of my arm," I said, but when I tried to fling his hand off me and my arm remained still, I realized just how strong Mike's grasp was.

"Listen to me. I never told you this, but Supreme was planning on signing with my label. While you were in the hos-pital he came over here and we talked. We were so close to negotiating a final deal. So see, Supreme would want me to have his music not Atomic records."

"You're a liar. Supreme couldn't stand you. He would have never given you his music." Mike's jaw muscle began to spasm as his patience wore thin.

"You have no idea everything I went through to make sure that music ended up in my hands. When I found out Supreme's contract was up with Atomic I tried every tactic to get him to come to the other side."

"You mean the dark side?"

"If you want to call it that, but every side in this here music game is dark. There is nothing innocent about it.

When you decide to enter this world you're checking your soul at the door, trust me. If you don't, you'll be eaten alive. Supreme had gotten so huge he started believing that the rules no longer applied to him. I had to show him differently."

"What do you mean by that?"

"You know what I mean. Don't stand here and tell me that it never crossed your mind that I was the one who was responsible for Supreme's death." I felt my blood pressure rising. Mike was justifying the fear that had been bubbling inside of me.

"You murdered Supreme?" I asked flatly.

"I didn't do it personally, but I hired the men that did," Mike admitted with no remorse.

"Then you might as well have pulled the trigger yourself. Those men were shooting to kill anyone in sight and that included me."

"Yes, that's true. From the moment I first saw you, I always wished you could've been mine, but with life it's all about timing. You were Supreme's wife, so if he had to go then so did you. But when you survived I thought maybe our time had finally come and we had a chance. You had everything I needed and wanted. Physically you are perfect, mentally we're one in the same, and you held the key to the power I craved. I was willing to be patient so I could have you all to my self.

"Of course we had our stumbling blocks when you dipped out with Jalen. I couldn't let some knuckle-head basketball player destroy all the work I had put in."

"Wait. That was you who had me tied up so your goons could almost beat Jalen to death? You're beyond a monster."

"You left me no choice. I warned you to stay away from him at the club, but being the stubborn person you are of course you ignored my advice and so did he. When I found out you were spending the night with him in some hotel I had to act fast. What if you started falling in love? Then there would be no room for me in your life. That was unacceptable."

"How did you know what hotel we were at?"

"Precious, why do you underestimate me? Nina was my mole. I hired her so I was always one step behind you and five steps ahead."

"Did you have Nina set me up?"

"No, she did that dumb shit all on her own. Falling in love can cause even the strongest woman to lose any sense of rational thinking. Nina fell hard for Nico, but he was still in love with you and she hated you for that. Nina wanted to put you six feet under on several occasions, but I made it clear that no one could harm you. After Supreme died I decided you would be my wife. But Nina let her hate toward you dictate her actions, and it didn't work out the way she planned."

"So was her relationship with Jamal a part of your scheme, too?"

"Good ol' Jamal, he was my back up plan. See I have inside people everywhere, and I knew that Supreme's contract had a tricky little clause. In the event of his death all of his music would automatically belong to Atomic records unless Supreme left behind a spouse or children. In that case his family would receive royalties to his music under contract and be sole owners of all existing music that wasn't under contract with Atomic at the time. Initially when I planned to kill both you and Supreme, I knew that Jamal would be the man with the power. With Nina being his wife, and the way she had that corny nigga wrapped around her finger, the power would then be hers.

"Obviously, plans changed and Jamal was no longer a key factor so Nina focused more on Nico. She felt it wasn't necessary to keep up her charade with Jamal. She never had any intentions of marrying him. But I tried to convince her to keep it going with him because I never knew when I would need Jamal for an important business deal. But Nina was dick whipped. She was running the streets closing heroin deals for Nico and plotting your death."

"So now what?" I asked dryly. Listening to Mike break down the madness had left me drained.

"Now, I have to kill you. I mean, I've revealed too many incriminating secrets, you're a liability."

"With me dead, you'll never get the masters."

"All is not lost. It also stipulated in Supreme's clause that if his spouse or children die then the rights will once again belong to Atomic unless another agreement has been signed relinquishing the rights to Atomic and going to another party or parties. Since I know you've haven't struck such a deal, then once again I'll go to my fallback plan and get Jamal in my pocket."

"You think you have it all figured out."

"That's what I do. But it's really all your fault. If you had just played your position we would be discussing wedding plans instead of how I'm going to kill you."

"Do what you have to do. Because trust your day will come, and we all know payback is a bitch."

"So they say. But I'm dealing the cards right now, and before I put you out of your misery I want something that you owe me."

"I don't owe you shit."

"Yes, you do. I've been waiting to get a taste of that pussy, and before you die, I will." Mike jumped up from the table and lunged toward me, knocking me and my chair to the floor.

"No the hell you won't!" I mustered all my strength and crawled from out of Mike's clutches, kicking him in the face. I made a quick leap toward my purse in a bid to retrieve my gun and hopefully save my life. I wasn't fast enough. Mike reached for my neck and latched onto the diamond necklace he had just put on me. He ripped the necklace off, cutting my neck. I lost my balance and slipped on the marble floor.

"Shit!" I yelled as my back hit the floor. Even with the agonizing, throbbing pain I extended my hand out trying to reach for my purse. It was no use. Mike pinned my arms down then lifted up my skirt and was clawing my body like a deranged beast.

"This pussy belongs to me," he groaned as he forced his penis inside of me and pounded on my body with each thrust. "You see what you made me do?" Mike continued, breathing heavily. I was boiling over in rage. I believe rape is the worst crime you can commit against a woman. A man is using his power to strip away a woman's right to say 'no'. He leaves her with no control, weak, because she is unable to defend herself. Now I wanted Mike dead for multiple reasons. I would've preferred him to put a bullet in my head than stick his dick inside of me. He was about to murder me twice. I felt his body vibrating against mine as he emptied himself inside of me. During his moment of weakness, with the metal heel of my 4-inch pumps, I stabbed Mike in the calf, getting my heel about 2-inches deep.

"Ahhh shit!" he groaned as he pulled my shoe out of his leg. Free, I slid from up under Mike, jumped up and got my purse. By the time Mike looked up he was staring down the barrel of my gun.

"Now what, motherfucker? Killing you will be my greatest pleasure yet. First I'ma shoot off one fucking nut at a time before I blast off your dick. Then, right when you're about to bleed to death I'll finish you off with a bullet between your eyes. I cocked my gun, ready to watch Mike's blood decorate the white marble floor. Suddenly, something came crashing through the windows and busting through the front door.

"Police! Everybody freeze! Ma'am, put your gun down." My first thought was whether I could squeeze one off in Mike before I put my gun down and make it seem like a mistake. That thought quickly ended when I realized that at least a dozen SWAT team cops were aiming straight at me. Still, I weighed my options. I didn't care if they killed me just as long as I killed Mike first. This was about more than just Supreme.

"This son-of-a-bitch raped me, and I want him to die." I played the sympathy card. Set on murkin' Mike, I at least wanted them to know why.

"Ma'am, please put down your gun. We can't do anything to help you until you put your weapon down."

I heard what the officer was saying, and I knew he was right, but Mike raping me kept replaying in my head and each time I got angrier and angrier. Then there was chaos amongst the officers, and I heard a familiar-sounding voice fighting its way into the room. "Sir, you need to leave. You shouldn't be here," said an officer.

"Precious, please put down the gun." My whole world stopped. "It's okay. It's over now." Mike and I were transfixed on him, both believing our eyes were playing tricks on us. But they weren't, what we were seeing was just as real as the gun in my hand. "Baby, please put down the gun, I'm begging you," he pleaded.

A rush of blood went to my head; my heart was beating so loud I felt like the whole room could hear it.

"Supreme, you're dead, how can you be standing there?"

"Just put down the gun, and I'll explain everything." My mind was moving forward, but my body was standing still. I was frozen in fear because I didn't want to let my heart believe that Supreme was alive and standing in front of me.

"Supreme, is that really you?" I stepped forward with the gun still in my hand. The cops followed my lead and raised their guns higher.

"Yes, now, baby, please put down the gun before they hurt you." He moved closer to me, and I could see the concern in his face. One of the cops standing between us raised his hands letting Supreme know not to take another step. I lowered my gun, removed my finger from the trigger and placed it on the floor. Quickly, the police filed in, checking every corner of the house.

In the midst of the chaos, Supreme ran up and lovingly wrapped his arms around me. I was still in shock and couldn't return his embrace. I could hear the police officer reading Mike his rights as he demanded to call his attorney. Handcuffed with his hands behind his back, he staggered past me and Supreme giving us the most diabolical look.

"We ain't finished, trust," Mike said with confidence dripping from his voice as if he didn't know he was about to be facing mad time in jail.

"Ma'am." The officer tapped me on my shoulder.

"That's Mrs. Mills," Supreme corrected him.

"Mrs. Mills, we need to take you to the hospital and have you examined." I nodded my head, agreeing with the officer. If the police couldn't get any other charges against Mike to stick, the rape case damn sure would. I wanted to follow all the necessary procedures to guarantee that.

Reason to Believe

Supreme remained right by my side during my visit at the hospital where a rape kit was performed and I was subjected to intensive questioning by the police. They grilled me about Nico, Nina's murder and my involvement with Mike. I was careful to give them as much detailed information as possible without self-incrimination. I did find it hard to focus because I still hadn't processed that Supreme was really alive.

"Mrs. Mills, we only have one more question for you, as I'm sure you're anxious to leave the hospital and go home," the officer said, trying to sound sympathetic.

"Yes, I am. But what's the question?"

"Do you have any idea where we can find Nico Carter?"

"No, I don't." It wasn't a lie. As far as I knew, Nico was long gone and I had no idea if and when he'd be back. "I also have a question for you." The officer looked up at me from writing something down on his notepad.

"Yes."

"How did you know I was at Mike's house?"

"You can thank your friend Jamal Crawford for that. He stopped by the precinct late this afternoon with his concerns. Jamal told us about the contract he had doctored up and that you believed you knew who killed Supreme. He had a bad feeling and for good reason. Jamal had no idea who might be involved, but we assumed from the information he gave us you knew it was Mr. Owens. We had been watching him for some time because of our suspicions about his involvement with the attempt on your husband's life. I wish we could've arrived sooner and prevented the rape, but I'm relieved we're not investigating another homicide. I know you have a lot more questions, but I'm sure your husband can explain the rest."

Supreme was holding my hand tightly as I stared at him. Our mouths weren't saying a word but our eyes were speaking volumes. He then opened the palm of my hand, and I saw the necklace that I had been gripping so tightly. It was the necklace Supreme had given me, what seemed like a lifetime ago, on the day I had been released from the hospital. I had let Mike take it off, but I was holding onto it for dear life, feeling that it was giving me strength. Supreme took it out of my hand and placed it back around my neck, where it belonged. After leaving the hospital we decided to stay at a hotel because if we went home Nathan and the rest of the security would have a million questions. Neither of us was ready for that.

On the drive to the hotel I just laid my head in Supreme's lap, taking in his scent, studying his hands—he was really with me in the flesh.

When we got in our hotel room, one of the first things Supreme did was turn on the water in the Jacuzzi. He bathed me from head to toe in the hot water. It was exactly what I needed to erase the foulness Mike had set on my body. After relaxing in the water for about an hour, Supreme dried me off and carried me to the bed. My exhaustion finally took over me, and I fell into a deep sleep in his arms.

When I woke up the next morning, Supreme was sitting in the chair wide awake. "How long have you been up?" I questioned.

"Since you fell asleep last night. All this time being away from you I dreamed of just watching you sleep. These last few months have been the hardest of my life."

"Tell me what happened," I said, needing to know the truth. Supreme stood up from the chair and sat down at the edge of the bed. I sat up giving him my full attention. He took a deep breath and began speaking.

"After you got shot and were in the hospital, Mike came to me offering a deal to sign with his record label. Of course I turned him down. He reached out to me a few more times afterwards, and I knew he was furious, but never did I believe he would resort to murder.

"When I was shot leaving the hospital with you, the doctors performed emergency surgery, and I was in critical condition, but they knew I would survive. They told you and everyone else I had died, following the orders of the police and the FBI."

"But why?"

"Because the FBI had been trying to build a case against Mike on drugs, money laundering and all sorts of other crimes for a minute. They had an informant in place who got word that Mike was responsible for the hit on me, but the FBI needed more proof. They wanted Mike to believe that I was dead to protect me until they had all the evidence needed to get an indictment and conviction."

"But...but I saw you die."

"So you thought.. But after they took me in for emergency surgery, what followed was all staged. Baby, you have no idea what the government can do. After they declared me dead and took me into hiding, the Feds transferred me to one of their hospitals, where they nursed me back to health. Having you and my parents grieving over me and watching mad people mourn my death when I was very much alive, that shit was hard. Harder than being shot seven times. Precious, I was watching the whole thing on TV from my bed. Even when you were crying over my casket, you looked beautiful. I wanted to reach through the television and hold you so you would know everything would be okay because I was alive. After my ordeal, I'm starting to question whether those Tupac rumors are true."

"So where were you for all these months?"

"In a safe house somewhere in Long Island. They had me stashed under lock and key. They kept me in the dark about how the investigation was going. A few police officers were with me 24/7 for protection but they wouldn't tell me shit. Luckily, I overheard one of them talking about the cops making their move on Mike because they believed you were in imminent danger. I told them if they didn't take me to you I would go on my own, and the only way to stop me was to kill me. They could see I was dead-ass serious, so they took me to you.

"I was stressing the whole time because I didn't know what the fuck was going on. All I knew was that you were with Mike. Baby, I'm so sorry I couldn't protect you from that piece of shit. I wanted to kill that nigga with my bare hands."

"I still can't believe you're alive. Since you've been gone my life has been on a downward spiral. I never thought I would touch you or hold you again. Or feel you make love to me. The only reason I wanted to live was to avenge your death."

"I know how hard it's been for you, baby. But I'm here, and starting right now we're making up for our lost time."

"Can we start by you making love to me?"

"Are you sure you're ready for that? After what happened with Mike I understand if you need time and want to wait."

"I want to forget about Mike and what he did to me. Today is a new beginning, and I want to share it with you. I need to feel you inside of me, so I'll know you'll never leave me again."

"Damn, Precious, you don't have to say no more. I've been wanting to feel what's mine for too long. I've missed you, baby."

"I've missed you, too."

Supreme and I made love, and for that moment everything in the world seemed perfect. My husband was home, and I finally had my life back.

Life After Death

The Present...

I had beaten too many odds not to be able to battle for the life of my unborn child. Yeah, I was having a difficult childbirth, but I was determined to bring a healthy seed into this world. My baby needed me, and I needed my baby even more. With all the bullshit I had been through in my young life, I could muster the strength to push my child out, and that's what I did. I took a deep breath and put my back and everything else into it, pushing out the gem I would love more than anything in this world, including myself.

"Precious, you did it," I heard both the doctor and nurse say in unison. But I didn't need them to say shit because the thunderous cries ringing in the air were the only announcement needed.

The doctor handed me my baby, and I was at a loss for words. It seemed like yesterday death was knocking at my door, when in fact it had been ten months since the end of my ordeal. Now here I was holding my greatest accomplishment.

"Precious, would you like for me to bring the father back in?" the nurse asked. I kept my head down and nodded "yes," not wanting to look away from my bundle of joy.

While in labor I demanded Supreme leave the room. His presence was just making a stressful situation worse. He was acting as if he was in more pain than me, and that shit was just physically impossible. It killed me how Supreme was so hardcore when he hit that mic, but was absolutely no help playing coach in the delivery room. It was all good though—his strengths in everything else he touched made up for it.

When Supreme walked in I glanced up and he had the most serene expression. As he got closer a smile crept across his face and pure happiness beamed from his eyes. I knew how much the birth of our child meant to him. "Baby, meet your daughter," I said as I handed her over to the proud father. "I want to name her Aaliyah after my mother, especially since she inherited her green eyes."

"Whatever you want, baby. You've given me the most precious jewel ever. The world is yours." I knew he meant that, too. We had been through hell and back to finally be a family, but it was all worth it. Our love was stronger than ever and unbreakable. Relishing my blessings made me reminisce about the past and how the end of one life brought about the birth of a new one.

"If you don't mind, can I have a moment alone with our daughter?" I said, looking up.

"Of course, Mrs. Mills," the doctor said as he and the nurse left the room.

"Supreme, can you leave, too?" his eyelids got heavy, and I knew he was taken aback by my request. "Baby, I'm not pushing you away, I just need some private time with Aaliyah...a little mother and daughter bonding. Please."

"I understand. I'll go call the family and let them know we welcomed a princess into the world today." He smiled. When the door shut behind him I released the tears that I had been holding back. There was still a part of me that I couldn't share with anyone else, including Supreme, but that had now changed. I could reveal my vulnerability to my daughter.

Aaliyah's eyes locked with mine as if she knew I needed her full attention when I purged my soul. "My beautiful baby, never did I believe I was worthy of something as precious as you. You were the one gift in life I felt was unattainable. I know that I don't deserve you, but God has granted me a second a chance in life, and I'm thankful. You will never have to experience the hell that I've gone through. I will protect you from the street life that almost destroyed me and your father.

"Holding a living creature that your blood runs through is the most potent rush in the world. My mother may have not been strong enough to fight back the powerful demons that corrupted the bond between mother and child, but my life now belongs to you. This is our first chapter, and I will turn over a new leaf, but if anyone tries to destroy what we share I will delete them from this earth—that I promise you. I will also teach you the necessary tools to survive in this world, because if you don't know evil you can never recognize good. People think your mother is a bitch, but trust you will be the baddest bitch ever." I swear I thought my eyes were playing tricks on me because all I saw was gums as Aaliyah gave me a smile. "That's right, my baby, with your beauty and charm they'll never see you coming until it's too late." I kissed Aaliyah on the forehead, anointing her the future Queen Bitch.

Epilogue

After the birth of our daughter, Supreme and I moved to California to get away for the drama that still surrounded us on the East Coast. We needed a change of scenery so we could concentrate on raising Aaliyah. Supreme didn't re-sign with Atomic Records. Instead, he put out his CD under his own label, Supreme Records. He titled what was supposed to be his last CD, "*Resurrection.*" It went double platinum within the first week and went on to be the biggest selling record that year. After its success Supreme had more money than he could ever spend in this lifetime or the next. He retired from being a rapper and focused on making major moves behind the scenes.

Nico still hadn't resurfaced even though the police had no intentions of charging him with the attempted murder of Supreme. He still hadn't contacted me, and I figured that once he got word that Supreme was alive he would think I'd go back on my word and cooperate with the police for his attempted murder against me. But I had no plans to do so. I told Supreme how Nina was this close to ending my life, but

Nico stood in front of me ready to take the bullet in my place. He understood that we had now washed our hands of the past and settled the score. I had the same cell number and prayed that one day Nico would call, and I could tell him it was all good for him to go home to Brooklyn.

When Maya found out that her brother Mike was not only responsible for the attempted murder on Supreme's life but that he also raped me, she completely turned against him. The tragic situation brought us even closer. During that time, Maya and Clip also got back together and finally let the world know they were in love. They moved to California together after Clip became the first artist signed to Supreme Records. His album is scheduled to drop right before Christmas.

Jamal eventually gave up on finding Nina's killer and focused all his energy on running Atomic Records. He eventually found love in the workplace. He is now engaged to his trustworthy personal assistant.

Mike hired the best attorney money could buy, determined to beat his case. He even tried to bargain with prosecutors by ratting me out for the murder of Antwon O'Neal. Unfortunately for Mike, he did such an excellent job of disposing of the body there wasn't any evidence to corroborate his story. The police felt it was a weak attempt to blow smoke so the prosecutors pursued their case and took Mike to trial. I sat in the front row of the courtroom when Mike was convicted and sentenced. He was given fifteen years for raping me and twenty-five years for the attempted murder of Supreme with his time running concurrent. He gave me an ice-cold glare and mouthed that he would be back for my life. I knew I was being met with the face of evil, but his threats didn't faze me. I was free of Mike and had my life back.

As for me, I felt stronger than ever. I had my baby and the love and support of my husband. With Supreme's encouragement I decided to enroll in college so I could obtain my degree. I always wanted to take my education to the next level but was afraid of failure. I no longer had those fears. I realized that the only person that can stop you from obtaining your dreams in life is you.

ORDER FORM
Triple Crown Publications
PO Box 247378
Columbus, OH 43224
1-800-Book-Log

NAME	
ADDRESS	
CITY	
STATE	
ZIP	

TITLES	PRICE
Cut Throat	$15.00
Dangerous	$15.00
Dime Piece	$15.00
Dirty Red **Hardcover**	$20.00
Dirty Red **Paperback**	$15.00
Dirty South	$15.00
Diva	$15.00
Dollar Bill	$15.00
Down Chick	$15.00
Flipside of The Game	$15.00
For the Strength of You	$15.00
Game Over	$15.00
Gangsta	$15.00
Grimey	$15.00
Grindin' **Hardcover**	$10.00
Hold U Down	$15.00
Hoodwinked	$15.00
How to Succeed in the Publishing Game	$20.00
In Cahootz	$15.00
Keisha	$15.00

SHIPPING/HANDLING
1-3 books $5.00
4-9 books $9.00
$1.95 for each add'l book

TOTAL $_____

FORMS OF ACCEPTED PAYMENTS:
Postage Stamps, Personal or Institutional Checks & Money Orders.
All mail-in orders take 5-7 business days to be delivered.

ORDER FORM

Triple Crown Publications
PO Box 247378
Columbus, OH 43224
1-800-Book-Log

NAME	
ADDRESS	
CITY	
STATE	
ZIP	

TITLES	PRICE
Larceny	$15.00
Let That Be the Reason	$15.00
Life	$15.00
Life's A Bitch	$15.00
Love & Loyalty	$15.00
Me & My Boyfriend	$15.00
Menage's Way	$15.00
Mina's Joint	$15.00
Mistress of the Game	$15.00
Queen	$15.00
Rage Times Fury	$15.00
Road Dawgz	$15.00
Sheisty	$15.00
Stacy	$15.00
Still Dirty *Hardcover	$20.00
Still Sheisty	$15.00
Street Love	$15.00
Sunshine & Rain	$15.00
The Bitch is Back	$15.00

SHIPPING/HANDLING
1-3 books $5.00
4-9 books $9.00
$1.95 for each add'l book

TOTAL $_____

FORMS OF ACCEPTED PAYMENTS:
Postage Stamps, Personal or Institutional Checks &
Money Orders.
All mail-in orders take 5-7 business days to be delivered.

ORDER FORM
Triple Crown Publications
PO Box 247378
Columbus, OH 43224
1-800-Book-Log

NAME	
ADDRESS	
CITY	
STATE	
ZIP	

TITLES	PRICE
The Game	$15.00
The Hood Rats	$15.00
The Pink Palace	$15.00
The Set Up	$15.00
Torn	$15.00
Whore	$15.00

SHIPPING/HANDLING
1-3 books $5.00
4-9 books $9.00
$1.95 for each add'l book

                                               TOTAL $_____

FORMS OF ACCEPTED PAYMENTS:
**Postage Stamps, Institutional Checks & Money
Orders, All mail in orders take 5-7 Business
days to be delivered**